SWEET REVENGE

A DEWBERRY FARM MYSTERY

KAREN MACINERNEY

GRAY WHALE PRESS

MYS
F MAC

Dedicated to the memory of Jelly Bean, the tiny abandoned chihuahua who hobbled into my heart and my life just a few short months ago. I'm sorry I couldn't find a way to make you well again, sweetheart, but I gave your fictional counterpart a better ending. (And thanks to you, I now have Iggy!)

Dedicated also to all the families whose roots lie in Texas, including those whose ancestors came here by force and those whose ancestors were forced to leave. Your stories deserve to be heard.

1

I don't know why nobody's done a horror film called "The Beekeeper" yet, but as I looked at myself reflected in the back window of my little yellow farmhouse, swathed in a beekeeper's hazmat-style suit with a smoking metal tin in my right hand, I reflected that I'd be a good candidate for the starring role.

"Got your gear on?" my friend and mentor Serafine asked. Unlike me, who had prepared for Bee Armageddon, Serafine had retained her flowy black sleeveless dress, only adding a veiled hat (also black) and gloves for protection.

"I look like I'm ready for a moonwalk," I said, adjusting my hat. "Are you sure you don't want to suit up?"

"The bees know I'm all right," she said. Since Serafine was not only a veteran beekeeper (she owned the Honeyed Moon Meadery just down the road), but the daughter of a voodoo priestess, I decided she knew what she was doing. She'd made a few concessions to the bees, at least; she'd eschewed the bright colors she favored and her usual floral perfume, lest the bees mistake her for a flower. It wouldn't be a hard thing to do; Serafine was beautiful, her smooth dark skin glowing in the early afternoon light, her high cheekbones lightly dusted with rose-gold blush that iridesced in the sun. "Ready?" she asked again, her almond-shaped eyes glinting with expectation.

"I guess," I said, not feeling quite as confident as I would have liked. I'd gotten the hang (mostly) of cows and goats, but bees were something else altogether. As much as I enjoyed watching the come and go from the hives I'd placed on the far end of my small peach orchard, opening an active beehive filled me with trepidation--even though we had picked the time of day when most of the worker bees were out foraging. It was June, after all, and wildflowers were still blooming, providing tons of nectar for my five fledgling colonies.

Serafine had helped me set them up back in early spring, from getting together my bee orders and selecting and locating the frames to putting out a water source for when Dewberry Creek ran dry. I'd noticed a drop in activity in two of the hives the previous week, so it was time to check on them, and Serafine, bless her, had offered to help me out. She'd come with her assistant, Chloe, who looked like her protégé in just about every way. Like Serafine, Chloe was dressed in a flowing dress, only hers was blue with gold stars sprinkled across it, and she wore her hair in small braids that swung around her young face as she moved. She even wore the same shade of rose-gold blush, it seemed... only the color didn't quite work against her milk-colored skin. Chloe hung back, playing with my slightly tubby apricot poodle Chuck, as Serafine and I advanced on the hives. The farm's new kittens, Smoky and Lucky, had adjusted nicely since I found them in the chimney and the old well, and Chuck had taken them on as if they were his own, often herding them when he felt they were straying too far. Now, they were busy stalking each other under my grandmother's pink roses; watching them roll around always brought a smile to my face.

"I always thought you could just let the bees do their thing," I said.

"They're livestock of a sort," Serafine said. "And livestock always needs tending."

"That certainly is true," I said, glancing over at the pasture, where my milch cow Blossom, her daughter, and my burgeoning herd of goats, led by Hot Lips, grazed. I milked them twice a day, kept them fed and watered, monitored their health, and made sure they weren't conspiring to tunnel through the fence. And then there were the chickens, who were adjusting to the addition of six new chicks. It was a full-time job just managing the animals on Dewberry Farm... never mind the rows of early summer vegetables and the peach trees I was attempting to keep from being plucked clean by birds and squirrels.

"It's these that are the problem, right?" she asked, casting an expert eye over the hives and immediately identifying the two that had seen a drop in activity.

"I think so," I said.

"Let's take a look," she said. I stood, frozen. She gave me a kind smile and deftly took the smoker from me. "Just do what I say," she said, "and stay calm."

As Serafine directed me (and held the smoker), I opened the first hive and pulled out one of the frames.

"Hmm," she said, pointing to the gaps in the comb. "See this area here? It's spotty. The flowers have been good, but the bees here aren't thriving."

"I see what you mean," I told her, looking at the comb.

"No eggs. Not a lot of brood cells or larvae either." She

tilted her head and listened. "The bees' pitch is a little high, too. I think you're missing a queen."

"That sounds bad."

"It's fixable," she reassured me. I replaced the frame gently and we moved onto the next hive, which was humming more comfortably. "This one looks just fine," she said. "When you're ready to harvest, you'll want to take from the sections where they're all capped off," she told me.

Although the smoke-dazed bees collected on the veil of my hat and the arms and legs of my suit, they seemed not to bother Serafine. When one flew onto her nose, she simply sang a little song to it--something with no words, but soothing nonetheless--and it flew off a moment later. Unlike me, who was vibrating with tension like a high-voltage line under the hot beekeeper's suit, she radiated peace and confidence, and the bees seemed to sense it.

It took a half hour to inspect all of the hives; Serafine diagnosed two of them as being queenless. The spring wildflowers had been lush this year, thanks to generous rains, and I was glad to see that most of the hives were filling with honey; it was amazing what these industrious insects could do. I wouldn't be harvesting honey this year--it was better for the bees to wait until the hives were more established--but I was looking forward to having my own honey and beeswax products to sell at market. Although if I was this stressed just checking the hives, I couldn't imagine how it would feel actually taking honey from them. Or, more to the point, how the bees would feel about my removing swathes of the comb they'd worked so hard to make. It took, after all, an entire lifetime for one bee to make a mere 1/12th of a teaspoon. Remembering how much work it took made the sweet taste all the sweeter.

"What do I do about the two queenless hives?" I asked

once we were far enough from the hives that I dared to take off my suit. Despite her lack of protective gear, Serafine had been stung only once, when she'd accidentally pressed a bee between her arm and her body. "Poor little thing," she'd cooed, removing the stinger from her skin and cupping the dying bee in her hand. I'd somehow gotten stung three times by bees who had snuck under my net hat, leaving me with a constellation of burning stings across my cheek and neck. My words hadn't been quite as generous as hers when it happened.

"I've got something to help with that," she said, digging in her voluminous purse. She pulled out a small tin, then popped the top off and offered it to me.

"What is it?"

"Calendula salve," she said. "It'll help the stings."

"Thanks," I said, taking a dab on a fingertip and touching it to my neck and cheek. It didn't take long for the sting to abate. "Wow," I said. "Where did you get this?"

"I made it," she grinned.

"Can I have the recipe? This stuff is magical!"

"I'm teaching a class on homemade salves and balms at Heritage Farm tomorrow," she said. "It's full, but since you're a friend, I can squeeze you in."

"I didn't know you were involved with the museum," I said. Buttercup's Heritage Farm Living History museum had opened a few months ago, with lots of support from Mayor Niederberger and the residents of Buttercup, particularly those who owned shops around the square. Priscilla Jordan-Melville, one of the wealthier residents of Buttercup, had donated a hundred acres of rolling pasture and woodland on Dewberry Creek for the project a few years back, along with a historic farmhouse that had been in her family for several generations; it had only recently opened. The director of the museum, Alicia Fawkes, was a charismatic and driven leader, with a strong push toward authenticity that from what I had heard had occasionally ruffled feathers among the board members, most of whom were from old Buttercup families.

Several antique farmhouses and barns in varying stages of decay had been moved to the site and restored, and historians from UT and Texas A&M, along with several craftsmen and craftswomen, had consulted on recreating a version of life as it once was in our neck of the woods. My friend Peter Swensen had given advice on their animal husbandry program, and both he and I had helped out in the gardens; just last week, we'd harvested the onion crop and hung the bulbs up to dry in the smokehouse.

"The seminar starts at six o'clock," Serafine said.

"I'll be there," I said. "I didn't know you were teaching classes!"

"Alicia is trying to expand the museum's offerings," she said. "One of the houses came from the Independence Colony."

"That was a freedmen's community, wasn't it?" I'd read about it in an article in the *Buttercup Zephyr* a while back.

"It was," Serafine said. "She's planning an exhibit on African-American history in the area, but some of the board isn't crazy about it."

"Why?"

"A lot of people would like to gloss over some of the more checkered parts of the area's past," she said with a sad smile. "There's been some resistance, but I'm guessing Alicia will manage to get it through. And I'm definitely in favor of it; I just found out I've got kin in the area."

"I thought you and your sister were from New Orleans!" I said.

"We are," she confirmed. " But I got curious about where our family might have come from originally, back in Africa —at least those that didn't come from Haiti. When I did the test, I got some info on where in West Africa we might have roots, but I also found out Aimee and I have got cousins just up the road in La Grange." Aimee was Serafine's sister, who lived and worked with her at the meadery.

"Part of your family was from Texas?"

"Looks like it," she said. "But nobody ever talked about it. I want to find out what happened."

"And you've got a lot of interest in the Independence Colony project, I'll bet."

"I do," she said. "I want to know how some of my folks got here, what life was like for them... and how they wound up coming to Louisiana from Texas. Or if maybe some of our kin moved here later."

"Have you met any of them yet?"

"Not yet," she said, "but I sent a few e-mails, and I've got a phone conversation set up for this weekend. I'm kind of nervous, to be honest. I'm kind of an unusual person... not to everyone's taste."

"Well, being the daughter of a voodoo priestess with a bit of the second sight isn't exactly ordinary," I said. "But I'm sure they'll love you."

"We'll see," she said.

"How come you didn't follow in your mother's footsteps, anyway?" I asked. I wasn't sure I was entirely comfortable with the whole voodoo thing, but I was very curious about it. Serafine must have had a very interesting upbringing, to say the least.

"I didn't feel called to it," she said. "My mother tried to get me to take over for her, but it wasn't for me; she ended up training one of my nieces instead. I still have all that she taught me, though... including some of what I'm going to be teaching tomorrow night."

"Really?" I asked.

"My mother knew all about medicinal herbs and treatments... that's what folks used to rely on for medical help... well, that and the *lwa*."

"The *lwa*?"

"The spirits," she said solemnly. "It's who folk petition for help. You don't mess around with the spirits, though, and you make sure to give them their due. My mother celebrated their birthdays, kept altars to them... they're linked to the saints, so their birthdays are often on saints' days."

"That sounds like a big commitment," I said.

"It is," she said. "It disappointed my mother when I didn't take over for her. Maybe my sister will pick it up one day. Who knows?" she shrugged. "I learned a lot from my mother, though, and I still pay my respects."

As she finished talking, Chloe and Chuck walked over.

"How did the check-up go?" Chloe asked.

"Most of the hives are fine, but two are struggling. She needs two new queens," Serafine said. "No mites, though."

"Thank goodness," Chloe said. "Those things are awful."

"I've heard," I said. Varroa mites were one of the beekeeping nasties of the world, and could wreak havoc on hives. "How's the internship going?" I asked her.

"Serafine's teaching me all about running the business," she said brightly.

"Chloe's taken over some of the social media already," Serafine said. "She's going to be taking pictures at the workshop tomorrow," she added, smiling proudly at the younger woman. "Maybe we can give Dewberry Farm a shout-out!"

"That would be terrific," I said. I'd started a page for the farm, but hadn't been very good about posting; maybe

Chloe's pictures would give me a boost. "The braids are a new look; I like them." Last time I'd seen her, her brown hair had been long and straight. "Where did you get it done?" I asked.

"Serafine braided it for me." She blushed, her hand darting to her new braids; she was obviously self-conscious about them.

"She's got lots of hair," Serafine said. "No extensions for this girl!"

"It suits you," I said.

"Thanks," Chloe said shyly.

Serafine's phone buzzed, and she glanced down at it. "I hate to run, but I've got to get back to the meadery," she said. "I promised Aimee I'd take over this afternoon."

"Thanks for coming out to check on the hives," I said. "And thanks for the invite to the workshop."

"My pleasure. I'll see you tomorrow!" she said. Chloe gave Chuck a good-bye scratch behind the ears before trailing her mentor back out the gate to the Honeyed Moon truck in my driveway. I waved as they headed down the drive, grateful to have supportive friends.

As I walked back to the house, a mooing sound came from somewhere off to my right.

Which was not a good thing, since the pasture was to my left.

I turned to see the goats trampling my neat rows of cucumbers and squash while Blossom and her daughter were starting to help themselves to my just-ripe peaches, ripping whole limbs off of my young trees in an attempt to get to the upper branches.

∾

"HEY!" I shouted, running toward the orchard and scattering Hot Lips and Gidget as I passed. Gidget looked up at me, a cucumber vine trailing from her mouth, and did a neat side-step right into a watermelon, which broke open under her sharp hoof. Blossom saw me coming, and trotted toward the creek. It wasn't back to the pasture, but at least it was out of the orchard. I glanced behind me to where the goats had resumed pillaging my garden.

There was only one goat left in the pasture; I ran to close the gate, and recoiled when I saw what was hanging about two fenceposts down.

It was a little doll with brown yarn hair, wrapped up in a scrap of red fabric, hanging upside-down on the fence post.

And stuck through the middle of it was a big, rusty nail.

2

It took an hour before I managed to get the animals all back into the pasture, using a batch of oatmeal cookies I'd made earlier in the week to lure them back in, then closing the gate behind them. They'd destroyed about a third of my cucumber crop, but I'd salvaged most of the peaches and tomatoes. I'd done a quick check of the fence; there were no holes. Either I hadn't latched it properly when I moved them from pasture to pasture earlier in the week, they'd figured out how to get the gate open themselves... or someone had opened it for them.

But what worried me more was the doll I'd found on the gate. How long had it been there? I hadn't been to this particular gate in days, so it could have been anytime in the past week, but even though I didn't want it to, my mind immediately leapt to Serafine, who had just left. She was the only person I knew who had any connection with voodoo, but I'd been with her the whole time she'd been on the farm, so I couldn't see when she would have had a chance to. And why would she? She'd been nothing but kind to me, helping me set up my hives and selling me beeswax at a good price to use for my crafting. I didn't know much about voodoo or anything like it, but I knew enough to know that whoever had nailed that doll to the fence didn't wish me well.

The thought sent a shiver through me.

Once the animals were in, I'd taken a picture of the thing, then eased it off the nail into a plastic baggie, being careful not to touch it, as if contact with it might burn me. On closer inspection, it appeared to be made of wax... probably beeswax, based on the honey color of it. Serafine obviously knew about voodoo, but had just told me she didn't participate in it. I knew she had some psychic abilities, but I'd never seen or heard her practicing it, other than letting me know my grandmother was there to support me and smudging the old Ulrich house not long after it had been moved to the farm.

I didn't know what to do with the thing--I didn't want it in my house or in my barn, or even my truck, so I left it my old smokehouse and debated what to do next. Should I call Serafine? Of all the people in Buttercup, she'd be most likely to be able to tell me what it meant. Then again, she was also the only person I knew of in Buttercup who had any experience putting things like that together. As fond of her as I was, a seed of doubt had sprouted in my heart, and I wasn't sure she was the person to ask.

THE GRAVEL PARKING lot of the Heritage Farm museum was half-full when I pulled in the next evening. As always, I felt like I'd gone back in time--except for the modern trucks and cars clustered by the entry, everything here looked like it belonged to a pre-industrial time.

Several wooden farmhouses in various stages of renovation were scattered on the grounds, along with three large barns--one of which, the structure closest to the entrance, had been turned into a crafting and workshop space. Two cows grazed in a nearby pasture, and a wooden fence contained neat vegetable gardens. I could see the empty rows where Peter and I had recently harvested onions and potatoes.

My eyes flicked to the most recent arrival to the museum, a small wooden house with a sagging roof and a breezeway in the middle, that I was guessing was the one Serafine had told me about. I was trying to remember what that style of house was called. It needed more than a little bit of work... and I knew from personal experience how much effort and money that might require. I had recently finished renovating a historic house I'd agreed to have moved to Dewberry Farm. I'd put it up on a few vacation rental sites about a week ago, but hadn't had many takers yet; I was hoping the addition of the living history museum might increase the number of folks interested in visiting Buttercup... and maybe staying at a historical house on a farm while they were in town.

As I walked through the front gate, I heard what sounded like an argument from one of the closer houses. I immediately recognized one of the voices as belonging to the chairman of the board. Priscilla Jordan-Melville, whose donation of the land had established the museum and whose very deep pockets had funded much of the restoration and construction efforts at the museum, was evidently not happy about something. I paused, curious as to what the problem was.

"There are a couple of things we need to discuss. First, I understand there have been a few missing items?" Priscilla said.

"Yes," replied the other woman, who I now realized was the museum director, Alicia Fawkes. "We're not sure if they've been misplaced or taken... I'm running a full inventory and conducting an investigation."

"Good," Priscilla said. "It's expensive to replace some of these items... and some of them are one-of-a-kind. My grandmother's thimble collection is irreplaceable."

"I'm sure we'll find it. I've been meaning to talk to you about your brother..."

"Yes. I appreciate you finding a job for him in the gift shop."

"Well, actually, it's not working out very well."

"No? Put him somewhere else, then. Groundskeeping?"

"He came in drunk yesterday morning and passed out in the storeroom," Alicia said. "I don't think the schools will be very happy if their children encounter someone who is... well, under the influence. Frankly, I'm not sure where else I can place him."

"I'm sure it was just an aberration. You'll find something. But I have something more important I'd like to discuss with you."

"Oh?"

"I have serious problems with this workshop you're running tonight. I just found out about it last week; it should have come up at the last board meeting?"

"Serafine is a local businesswoman," said Alicia. "She's well versed in home crafting and herbal remedies. Besides, I'm the director; I'm supposed to direct the programs."

"Herbal remedies? Sounds like witchcraft to me," Priscilla bit out.

"All of the herbs Serafine will be discussing were used by our ancestors, when access to medical care wasn't regularly available. I did the research myself."

"I think it's risky to give out snake oil recipes. It could be a legal liability."

"They're not snake oil recipes; they're historically based remedies," Alicia objected, "and a lot of them have a scientific basis. If you're that concerned, we can have the participants sign waivers. Besides, she's talking about topical arthritis relief using plants, not ingesting hallucinogenics or performing surgery."

"Peddling old wives' tales is not what this museum is about," said Priscilla. "Anyway, on another topic, I also have a huge issue with the purchase of the house from the Independence Colony; I plan to take it up with the board."

"It's an excellent example of a dogtrot house, and is part of our history," answered Alicia. Ah yes, that was the name. Dogtrot houses consisted of two small (usually one-room) cabins built with a breezeway between them; they were a historic building style that allowed folks to find respite from the sweltering summer heat before air conditioning and electric fans were an option.

"But the Independence Colony isn't part of Buttercup. It's twenty miles down the road."

"The Orzak house came from Round Top," Alicia said. "That's just as far. We chose to move the Warren house here not just because it's a dogtrot house, which is a classic southern house design style, but because that house and the people who lived there are part of our town's story."

"No they're not. They're part of the Independence Colony story."

"The family who built the Independence Colony house originally lived in Buttercup; they moved to the colony after emancipation. I think it's not just appropriate, but necessary if we're going to represent ourselves as documenting the history of Buttercup."

"This museum is about the residents of Buttercup."

"You mean the Anglo, German, and Czech residents of Buttercup," the director said, her voice edged with anger.

"That house didn't come from Buttercup," Priscilla repeated. "And I'm not okay with you advancing your own agenda. This is not your museum."

The director's voice was flat. "It's not my own agenda. It's historical fact."

"Look," Priscilla said. "You are here at the discretion of the board. The board chooses the direction of the museum. Not you."

"But..."

"You have been hired to carry out the board's directive. I'm calling a meeting this week. From now on, all new exhibits, acquisitions and workshops must go before the board for approval."

"You don't have the power to do that," Alicia retorted.

"I'm the chair of the board and my family's trust provides more than half your funding," Priscilla said in a chilly voice. "I think you'll find that I very much do have the power to do that. And if you want to keep your job, I'd recommend you remember it."

"But..."

"We'll talk after the board meeting," Priscilla said dismissively.

I turned to latch the gate behind me and had started walking toward the workshop barn when Priscilla strode out from behind the little stone house. Her back was erect, her highlighted straight hair artfully arranged around her impossibly chiseled, high-cheekboned face. She wore tight blue jeans, an expensive silk blouse, and cork wedges; a large diamond pendant glinted against her tan skin. I caught a whiff of expensive perfume as she breezed past me, giving me a tight smile as she headed toward a young man and a young woman who were standing near the chicken coop.

From behind her came Alicia, who was dressed in the long skirt and puffy blouse of a woman from the 1800s, her black hair pulled up in a tight bun from which a few strands had escaped. Her normally smiling face was drawn, and her eyes glinted with anger as she watched Priscilla disappear into the workshop barn.

"Hey," I said.

"Oh, Lucy, hi," she said, her face relaxing slightly when she saw me. "I hope you didn't hear all of that."

"I caught the end of it," I admitted. "Sounds like a tricky situation."

"I'm so mad I could spit," she told me. "That woman... I can't believe she wants to rewrite history."

"What do you mean?"

"I don't know how much you heard, but you know we just moved the Warren house to the museum, right?"

"I do," I said.

"Well, that house belonged to an African-American family that built a home in the Independence Colony."

"I've driven by that place," I said. There wasn't much there now other than cows, unfortunately; the only sign of the community that had once stood there was a few falling-down wooden houses and the remains of a church, its cross still standing atop its leaning roof.

"Well, the people who built that house were descended from a family that lived in Buttercup. Their ancestors were enslaved people who most likely picked cotton for local farmers."

"So there is a connection to Buttercup," I said.

"Exactly. And since African-Americans made up almost a quarter of the population of Buttercup at one point, it seems only right that their story should be part of the museum. Don't you think?"

"Seems reasonable to me," I said. "So what's the problem?"

"The problem is, I think Priscilla would rather tuck that part of history under the rug and stick to the 'Good Old Days' theme."

"Ah," I said, watching Priscilla with the two young adults by the coop; the young woman was looking at her phone, and the young man with her was staring off into the middle distance while Priscilla spoke to him. Neither of the two seemed to want to be there. "That's why she's calling the board meeting. Who are those two people she's with?"

"Her son, Damian, and his girlfriend," she said. "They're bored to tears unless it's something they can Instagram. The girl is some kind of influencer, apparently." As I watched, the young woman, a slender thing in a stylish sundress and hair that was a darker version of Priscilla's, held out her phone for a selfie and simpered in front of the coop. Her boyfriend watched with a bored look on his face, nodding as his mother pointed to the little dogtrot house. The girlfriend took a few more pictures and then hooked his arm, pulling him away. Priscilla watched them go, a petulant look on her beautiful face, then strode toward the Jordan house, which was the grandest of the historical houses and had pride of place in the center of the museum. I hadn't been shocked to discover it had belonged to Priscilla's family.

"What does her son have to do with the museum?"

"Nothing, thank goodness. At least nothing yet. Apparently he got a internship at a law firm in Austin, and keeps applying to law school, but his LSAT scores and his grades are... well, less than ideal. I keep waiting for Priscilla to ask me to make a job for one of them. Since nepotism seems to be the order of the day around here."

"Lucky you," I said. Neither of them seemed particularly enthralled by the museum's offerings; I couldn't imagine they'd be eager employees. "Let's hope you're wrong."

"In the meantime, though, what am I going to do about her?" Alicia asked. "I'm afraid she's going to nix the exhibit. I'm a historian; I can't stand by and let someone erase a part of history they're not comfortable with. It's unethical."

"I can see how you'd feel that way."

"Yeah. And valuable artifacts have been disappearing lately, and she's suggested she thinks I'm stealing them. I'm not the only one with keys to the place!" She took a breath and then kept going. "And then there's her brother, Arthur. He comes in only half the time, I have to redo everything he touches, and he's drunk more often than not. He's here tonight, 'helping' set up. You'll see what I mean."

"Rough day," I said.

"Rough week." She glanced at her phone. "Shoot; I've got to go help Serafine set up. Arthur is supposed to be doing it, but he's useless. I'm really eaten up about the Warren house; it's a perfect addition to the museum, and she's going to tank it before I even get it finished. I've even found the descendants of the family who built it."

"Really? That's amazing!"

"I know! A few of the Warren family are still in LaGrange. I promised them they could come to the grand opening, and they were kind enough to give me some family artifacts to include in the exhibit. I don't know what to do."

"I don't know what you can do," I said. "Except make your case to the board."

"Priscilla owns the board," she groaned. "I'm afraid it's a lost cause."

"All you can do is try," I said. "It might be worth contacting Mandy down at the *Buttercup Zephyr*... maybe if she ran an article on the house, it would be harder for the board to cut the exhibit?"

"Or easier for Priscilla to fire me." She sighed. "Still, it might be worth it. It makes me so mad, with her self-righteousness... like just because she has money she can do whatever she wants... people like that don't deserve the power they have." For a second, her features contorted into a look of rage I'd never seen in Alicia's sweet, dimpled face before, and then she remembered she had an audience. "I'm so sorry," she said, composing herself. "I'm just... it infuriates me, and I feel helpless to do anything about it."

"If there's anything I can do to support you, let me know," I said. "I think you're doing the right thing."

"Thanks. I'm afraid I'll need a miracle," she said. "Like maybe a tractor trailer squashing her little white BMW." Her hand leapt to her mouth. "Oh my gosh. I can't believe I just said that."

"It's okay," I said, putting a hand on her arm. "You're angry. I get it."

"I've got to pull myself together and go print some waivers," she said. "See you at the workshop?"

"I look forward to it," I said, and as Alicia hurried to the little house that functioned as the office, I followed the trail of Priscilla's perfume to Serafine's workshop.

Although the barn's exterior looked like any other agricultural building on the land, the interior of the barn had been transformed into a learning space that reminded me a little bit of the one-room schoolhouses of the past, only with long tables and metal folding chairs in lieu of the traditional desks. A galvanized tub of ice with bottles of Serafine's herbal tea sat near the door; I grabbed one, thankful for the cool drink in the June heat. At the front of the barn, Serafine had set up a table with a propane stove, several jars of herbs, beeswax, pots and wooden spoons, as well as several small mason jars. Each table was set up with its own stove, along with a smaller selection of what was on the table in the front.

The tables were all filled, mainly with women, but with a few men scattered among the participants, including Peter Swensen, my fellow farmer, who was seated with my good friend Quinn. I spotted a middle-aged man with a hangdog look and a stained button-down shirt that was hanging over the edge of his jeans listlessly arranging chairs; his name tag said Arthur Graham, and I guessed that must be Priscilla's brother. Also in attendance was Priscilla's handsome husband, Nigel Melville, who was talking to his wife in the back of the room. Although I couldn't hear what they were talking about, their faces looked strained, and I couldn't help but notice that he wasn't wearing a wedding band. Curious, I edged closer, taking a seat near the back of the barn.

"You can't fire someone for doing their job," he was saying.

"I'm the one who makes up the job description."

"Just like you decide everything else. You're only happy when you have people on a leash, begging for treats."

"That's a load of crap," Priscilla said in a very unladylike voice.

"Uh huh. That's why you organize everything so that you and your money dictate the terms. The museum, the Heritage Society... your brother... our son... and our marriage."

"You knew I was rich when you married me."

"I didn't marry you for your money. But I didn't know you'd use it as a cudgel, either."

"Cudgel? I gave you everything you wanted," she said.

"As long as I wanted what you wanted. I didn't want a mansion in the country.... I didn't want to move to Buttercup at all. And I certainly didn't want to paint the bedroom pink."

"Damask rose," she corrected him. "Well, it's a good thing you didn't marry me for my money," she hissed. "Because you're not getting any."

"I don't need your money. I have my own business."

"*Your* business? Last I checked, Texas was a community property state."

"You're not entitled to my business."

"Save it for my attorney," she spat. "And speaking of business, stay out of my mine."

"I'm going to do my damndest to keep you from turning this place into some kind of pioneer Disneyland," he said.

"I can do whatever I like," she said, drawing herself up. "And there's nothing you can do to stop me."

3

*N*igel stood and watched as Priscilla turned and stalked out of the barn on her wedges. His handsome face was flushed red and his nostrils flared; he was breathing hard. He was angry... very angry. He turned and darted his eyes at Serafine, who had been watching the exchange from the front of the room. He gave her a slight nod, and she dipped her head in response. Serafine and I weren't the only one who had observed the whole thing, though; so had Priscilla's brother, Arthur, who was sipping at a bottle as he leaned against one of the posts, watching with bloodshot eyes. I now noticed Chloe, who had been watching from a darkened corner, too, with a look that was nothing short of adoration and longing. Now that Priscilla was gone, she hurried over.

"Can I get you something to drink, Nigel?" she said. "That looked stressful."

"I've got a drink, thanks," Nigel said in a kind but dismissive tone, lifting a tea bottle, and he slid into a seat at the table next to mine, evidently ready to participate in the workshop. Which surprised me, really; I didn't see him as a do-it-yourself salve-maker type. Then again, who was I to judge? All I knew about him was that he was married to Priscilla and that he lived in Buttercup; I had only met him a couple of times at social gatherings. He did seem invested in the museum, based on what I'd just heard.

"If you change your mind..." Chloe said hopefully.

"I'm fine," he said, sounding a bit curt. Chloe lingered for a moment near his table, twisting her braids and looking like she was hoping he would initiate more conversation, before drifting reluctantly back to the front of the room, where Serafine was about to start the workshop.

"Everybody ready?" she asked. When the room murmured assent, she continued.

"Today, I'm going to show you how to make a few remedies that folks used to use when doctors were a little harder to come by," she announced. "There's a lot of wisdom in traditional cures, even though a lot of them are forgotten; you'd often find gardens with medicinal herbs on the old homesteads, and we've got a demonstration garden here, if you'd like to take a look after the workshop.

"For the salve, we're going to start by melting some beeswax," she continued, and I soon forgot about all the drama as I fell into the flow of creating something wonderful. Serafine led us through the process of making herb-infused oils and incorporating them into healing balms, including one with arnica for bruises and strained muscles, one with ginger, cayenne, and willow bark for arthritis, and the balm she had given me for the bee stings, which incorporated comfrey, yarrow, and the leaves of a weed I often pulled out of the garden, plantain--a small, leafy plant with long leaves, not to be confused with the oversized banana-shaped fruits I often saw in the grocery store.

It was a wonderful workshop, but neither Arthur nor

Nigel stayed the whole time. Arthur slid out a side door as soon as Serafine started, already reaching for his pocket--a flask?--and Nigel stayed only through the first project, bee sting balm, before heading out.

By the time we were done, I had learned how to infuse oils and had not just my own tin of bee sting balm, but recipes for calendula oil for winter skin care and a chamomile spray for sunburn.

"You should write a book," I told Serafine as Chloe cleaned the equipment off the tables and Serafine finished fielding questions from the animated workshop partici-pants. Alicia had showed up about thirty minutes in, just watching from the back of the room, before disappearing again. Would she tell Serafine what Priscilla had said to her? I found myself hoping not.

"I'm not sure they'd want all the remedies I've learned," Serafine said. "Like cow manure tea for arthritis, for example..."

"Umm... no," I said. "Probably not. But you wouldn't get any objection to honey, I'll bet."

"Oh, honey's good for a lot of things," she said. "Antibac-terial, antifungal... it's good for coughs, too."

"And better smelling than manure tea... or an onion poultice," I said. "My grandmother swore by those onion poultices; I got a summer cold one July, and she made me keep one on my chest for hours. It was enough to make me pretend I wasn't sick."

Serafine laughed. "I get that. And don't get me started on kerosene... my grandmother called it 'coal oil.'" She shivered. "Topical is okay, but a spoonful at night? It doesn't matter how much sugar you add to it, it's still kerosene."

"Wait. You had to swallow kerosene as a kid?"

"Every time I went to grandma's house," she said.

"I will never complain about liver and onions again," I told her. She laughed. "Thank you so much for teaching this workshop; I was thinking of expanding my market offerings, and I was considering adding a few salves and balms."

"Once you get your hives going, that'll be easy," she said. "Good use of beeswax; in the meantime, I can supply a little more if you need."

I was about to ask her about the doll I'd found at the farm, but something held me back. Things were good between us, and I didn't want to muddy the waters by suggesting she'd had something to do with it.

Before I had a chance to decide what to do, Quinn came up to us. My carrot-topped friend looked bright and cheerful; ever since Jed Stadtler, her abusive ex, had been jailed a year or so back, she'd blossomed. Some of it could be attributed to her relationship with Peter Swensen, who was Jed's polar opposite, but that wasn't all of it. It's hard to bloom when you live in fear all the time.

"Great workshop, Serafine," she said. "And this honey lemon tea is terrific." She lifted a bottle of tea that must have come from the galvanized tub at the door of the barn.

"I'm glad you like it," Serafine said. "I'm hoping everyone else does, too. I'm trying to expand the business beyond alcoholic beverages, and we southerners love our tea."

"But there's something different about this I can't put my finger on. Something herbal and zingy... what is it?"

Serafine smiled. "Trade secret. It's a mix of herbs, actually. Lemon verbena, mint, and a few other things."

"It's delicious, whatever it is," she said. "If you can get this into the stores, you'll be a millionaire."

"Let's hope H-E-B takes it," she said. H-E-B was a huge Texas grocery store chain, and I knew it was highly competitive. "I pitched them last week, and I'm waiting to hear back."

"Ooh. Fingers crossed," I said. "Speaking of marketing, are you sure it's okay if I make some of these salves for sale at the market?"

"Of course!" she said. "I'm focused on the beverage industry, not personal care."

"If you'd like to sell some of your tea, let me know; I'm happy to bring a cooler for it."

"Would you? That would be terrific," she said. "Thanks, Lucy."

"Um... Serafine, we probably need to get going," Chloe said, twisting her braids. "I promised I'd help Aimee with Instagram tonight."

"Oh. Thanks, Chloe... you're probably right. I'll drop off some tea tomorrow, okay? How much do you want? It doesn't need to be refrigerated."

"Let's start with fifty," I told her. "I'm happy to put out some signage too, if you like. Just let me know how to price it and I'll keep track!"

"Thanks," she said as she gathered the rest of her supplies, putting them into a basket. As she did, the director of the museum walked up.

"Thank you again for doing the presentation," Alicia said. She hesitated for a moment, and I saw something flicker in her eyes... defiance? "Would you be willing to do another one soon? Maybe on traditional home remedies?"

"I'd love that," she said. "It's like paying tribute to my grandmother, passing on her wisdom. Thank you for the opportunity."

"My pleasure," she said. "Thanks again for coming. Do you need help getting out to your truck?" She looked around. "Arthur!" she called. "He was here just a minute ago... he was supposed to help with clean-up, but he just disappeared."

"I've got my trusty assistant here, so it's no problem," Serafine told her. "Okay, I'll see you tomorrow with that tea then," she said, addressing me. "And talk with a beekeeper friend of mine over in Smithville and have him send you some new queens; let me know if you need help requeening."

"I'm sure I will," I said. As Serafine turned to go, Alicia thanked me for helping out with the gardens. "Without you and Peter, I don't know what we'd do."

"Happy to help out. And I really hope the Warren house exhibit goes ahead after all. Any way I can get a sneak preview?"

"Absolutely," she said. "I've got to check on something in the office, but why don't you head down? Just let yourself in; it's stable enough now that I'm not worried about the roof caving in."

"That's comforting," I said. "Want to come with me?" I asked Quinn; Peter had left a few minutes earlier, doubtless to tend to his evening chores.

"Sure," she said as we left the barn and walked out into the museum grounds. "I've read about dogtrot houses, but I've never been in one. Why are they called that, anyway?"

"I don't know," I said, looking at the small log house. "I imagine sitting in that breezeway in summer was a lot better than being inside, though." As we walked down to the cabin, I thought I spotted something moving in the trees to my right. Was it Priscilla's brother? A deer, maybe? I stared into the undergrowth, but didn't see anything else. Maybe I'd been imagining it.

"Oooh," Quinn said as we stepped up onto the covered porch that linked the two cabin-style rooms a few minutes later. "It really does catch the breeze, doesn't it?"

"As long as it's oriented correctly, and this one is." Most

breezes in our part of the world were southeasterly, and before air conditioning, houses in the south were usually built to catch those breezes--and amplify them, with more expensive homes including porches, tall windows, and transom windows above interior doors to allow air flow.

The rough floor of the breezeway was pocked with dents and worn down from years of use; there were a few scorch marks on the weathered wood, and the boards were uneven. A few had been replaced with reddish cedar planks during the renovation; with time, I knew, they would turn the same gray as the rest of the planks.

"When was this place built?" she asked.

"Second half of the nineteenth century, I think," I told her.

"I wonder how many people lived here?" she asked, opening the door to one of the two cabins. Inside was a rough-hewn wood bed covered with a mattress--I could see the straw sticking out of the side--draped with what appeared to be an antique quilt.

"This must have been the sleeping quarters, based on the bed. I have no idea how many people slept here, though," I said. "Families were big back then. I'm sure some-body slept up in the loft," I suggested, pointing up toward a small platform in the rafters. A ladder leaned against the far wall, next to a small wavy-paned window.

"No air conditioning, probably no plumbing, a fire for cooking and heat... it was like camping full-time, wasn't it?"

"Only with occasional raids by the Comanches," I said. "And dresses that covered you from head to toe, even in the heat of summers."

"Plus corsets," Quinn grimaced. "I watched that Pioneer House reality show once. The men got do all the building and the fun stuff, but the women just stayed home and cooked, cleaned, did laundry and sewed clothes."

"Not to mention working in the fields," I said. "Thank goodness for washing machines and clothing stores. I don't mind the cooking, though."

"It helps to have an actual stove," she said.

As I touched a chink in the log walls, I said, "I just hope Alicia is able to pull off this exhibit."

"Why wouldn't she?" Quinn said. "Except for the roof, the place is in good shape."

"I overheard a conversation between her and Priscilla Jordan-Melville," I said, and told her what I had heard.

"That's not right," Quinn said. "You can't just dictate what the director does!"

"Priscilla donated all the land, she's on the board, and evidently she's going to do her best to do just that," I said as we exited the first cabin and stepped back out onto the breezeway. The second door was latched from the outside, which I thought was kind of odd. I opened the latch, then turned the door handle to the second cabin-room. The door didn't move when I pushed on it. "Something's blocking it, it seems."

"Let me help," Quinn said. Together, we pushed on the door; I could hear something slide over the rough floor on the other side of it. "Oh, God," Quinn breathed suddenly.

"What?" I asked.

"Look," she said, taking a step back and pointing.

Through the crack in the door I could make out a bit of blue denim. And below it, a stretch of tanned calf, ending in a cork wedge sandal.

There was a body on the other side of the door. And unless I was mistaken, it belonged to Priscilla Jordan-Melville.

4

"*P*ush harder," I said. Together, we shoved the door open enough for us both to slip inside. The cabin was stifling hot, and smelled of old wood and must and smoke and expensive perfume.

Priscilla's perfume.

"What's wrong with her?" Quinn breathed as I squatted down next to the slender woman's prone form. She was crumpled on the floor against the door, her neck at an awkward angle; her straight, highlighted hair was strewn in a rumpled halo around her head. I put my fingers on her neck, searching for a pulse.

There wasn't one.

"She's not breathing, and I can't get a pulse," I said. "Call 911."

As Quinn dialed, I straightened Priscilla's body and tilted her head back so I could do CPR. Her skin was still warm; I was hoping there was a chance I could revive her. I could hear Quinn talking with the dispatcher as I breathed air into her lungs, shuddering at the taste of her lipstick, and then pumped her chest, hoping I could bring her back. By the time the paramedics arrived, I'd been working on her for almost twenty minutes, and she still wasn't breathing.

"We'll take over from here," a young woman in blue told me. I stepped back from Priscilla's body, glancing for the first time around the small room. The only piece of furniture in it was an unfinished oak table; on top of it, all but empty, was a bottle of Serafine's honey tea.

"I'm not getting a pulse," the paramedic said, and looked up at me. "How long did you do CPR?"

"From the time we called," I said.

Quinn and I exited the small cabin as the paramedics retrieved the defibrillator and tried to shock her body back to life. After the fourth time, I heard the woman say, "It's not working."

"What do we do?" asked the middle-aged man with her.

"I think we need to call the police," she said.

"She's awfully young for a heart attack," the man said. "Think we should call the coroner, too?"

"We'll leave that to the police," she replied.

Quinn and I looked at each other, wide-eyed.

Priscilla was dead. The door had been locked from the outside when we got there. Was it an accidental death due to heat exhaustion or some hidden medical condition?

Or had someone killed her?

"SHOULD WE TELL ALICIA?" Quinn asked as we sat on the end of the porch, swinging our legs over the side as we waited for the police to talk to us; Deputy Shames had arrived not long after the paramedics, and she'd asked us to stay outside and wait. I was glad it wasn't Sheriff Rooster Kocurek, who had a nasty habit of wanting to arrest the wrong person (including me) and was not my favorite Buttercupian, to say the least.

"It's her museum, so we probably should," I said, wishing I had some of Serafine's honey tea to wash the bitter taste out of my mouth... I'd noticed it after I stopped giving Priscilla CPR. "I wish we'd gotten there earlier," I said, feeling suddenly exhausted. I was tired from administering CPR, but also upset that I hadn't been able to save her. "Maybe I could have revived her."

"She was gone when we got there," Quinn said. "There's no way to know how long she was like that."

"It can't have been too long," I said. "She was in the barn at the beginning of the workshop. What I don't understand is, how did that door end up latched? And why?"

"You're right; that is weird," Quinn said. "Maybe it just slid down accidentally when she closed the door?"

"Maybe," I said. It was possible, since it was one of those simple latches you lift and lower; it's possible that it was jolted when the door closed, and slid down to latch. It didn't seem likely, though.

"Did you see her fingernails?" Quinn asked.

"No," I said. "I wasn't looking."

"They were all torn, like she was scratching at the door trying to get out."

I shivered. It was a horrible thought.

"Do you think someone really might have killed her?"

"I don't know," I said. "She was arguing with her husband just before the workshop started. And she had it out with Alicia earlier, too."

"You were telling me," Quinn said. "She certainly made herself popular. Do you think any of them were mad enough they might have killed her?"

"Maybe," I said. As I swung my feet beneath me, I looked

over at the small cluster of trees next to the cabin; the sun was now low in the sky, and there were deep shadows beneath the foliage, but I caught a flash of color that didn't seem natural. I squinted into the dim light. There was a scrap of fabric hanging from one of the lower branches. I slid off the porch and walked over to it; it was another one of those little beeswax dolls. This one was crudely crafted and hung upside-down by a piece of twine. It swayed slightly in the breeze, and my stomach turned over.

Who had put this here?

"What's that?" Quinn asked when I came back to the porch.

"It kind of looks like a voodoo doll," I said. For some reason, I didn't share that I'd found one at my own farm just the day before. I hadn't wanted to blame Serafine for it, but twice in two days I'd found one... and both times she had been in attendance.

"Maybe Serafine put it up here to warn Priscilla off of moving the house again," Quinn suggested.

"Why would she do that? Alicia was the one who argued with her about that, not Serafine."

"Maybe Alicia told Serafine what was going on," she said. "Maybe she was putting some kind of protective magic on the place."

"I don't think she does that stuff," I said.

"Didn't she tell you she came from a long line of voodoo priestesses or something?"

"She does," I told her. "But we've talked about it; her family worked with it, but Serafine doesn't practice. She learned about it from her mom, and she's got some psychic abilities, but she's a businesswoman, not a rootworker."

"Rootworker?"

"She told me that's a better word for it than voodoo

priestess. I'm not totally clear on what it means--something about working with plants and spirits--but I don't think Serafine's responsible for putting this thing here."

"Who else in Buttercup would do something like that?" Quinn asked.

I sighed and glanced back at the dogtrot cabin. "That's the question, isn't it?"

"Oh," Quinn said. "I heard something this afternoon at the cafe. Someone in from LaGrange said that the Warren house is known to be haunted."

"Haunted? Why?"

"A man named Garland Sims disappeared one summer night in the 40s or 50s. Completely vanished. His family left the house not long after... it was a bad luck house, they said. They were one of the last families in the Independence Colony, and the whole place kind of turned into a ghost town after that."

"Any idea what happened to him?"

"He'd been accused of some kind of crime, according to what I overheard. He'd been acquitted in court a few days earlier, but the rumors were that some vigilantes came and dispensed their own version of justice. He was never seen again... and he was a young man, in his early twenties. But the family never heard a peep after the night he vanished."

"That's terrible," I said. "Maybe he got scared and ran?"

"Could be," she said, "but I think the vigilante option is more likely."

I sighed. I knew things like that had happened in the area, but it was hard hearing about it.

"Should we take that weird doll down?"

That question was answered when Deputy Shames emerged from the door of the cabin and walked over to us. "I understand you two found the body. I'd like to ask you a few questions."

"Sure," I said, and Quinn and I got up from the porch. "Where do you want us?" I asked.

"Right here is fine," she said, and as she pulled out her tablet, her eyes locked on the little doll dangling in the tree. "What's that?" she asked.

"I don't know," I said. Quinn and I exchanged glances as Deputy Shames took the steps down off the porch to take a closer look.

"Some kind of doll, looks like." She turned her intelligent eyes to us. "Is this part of the museum exhibit?"

I shrugged. "I don't know," I said.

"I'm bagging it," she said. She took two photos and then slipped it into a plastic bag she pulled out of her pocket. "You never know what might be relevant." She studied the doll for a moment and made a note, then turned back to us. "What were you two doing down here, anyway?"

"I hadn't seen the new house yet, so I asked the museum director if we could get a preview. She said yes." I told her about walking through the first room, then discovering that the second was locked.

"What do you mean, locked?" she asked.

"The latch had fallen down," I said. "It's the kind where you lift it to open the door, then slide it down into place to lock it."

"Why was there a lock on the outside of the door?" she asked, puzzled.

"I imagine it was padlocked shut at some point," I said. "Otherwise, I don't know."

"So the latch was down." She walked over to the door, donned gloves, and closed it. The latch didn't budge. "I'm not sure how that could have happened by accident."

"I don't know," I said, feeling a little bit sick to my stomach. Had someone locked Priscilla in?

"What happened to her, Deputy Shames?" Quinn asked.

"We're waiting for forensics to show up," she said.

"So you think it's a suspicious death."

"She was relatively young and in good health, and she was found dead in a locked room. That sounds suspicious to me," the officer said.

"Good point," Quinn said.

"I understand you administered CPR until the paramedics arrived," Deputy Shames said, addressing me.

"I did," I said.

"How was she situated when you entered the room and found her?"

"She was pushed up against the door," I said. "We had to shove hard to get in."

"It looked like she might have been trying to get out," Quinn said.

"What makes you say that?" the officer asked.

"Well, she was right by the door, of course. But I noticed her fingernails," Quinn said. "They were all messed up, like she'd been scratching at the door."

"I'll take a look at the inside of the door later," she said. "Did the two of you see her at any point this evening?"

"She was in the barn before the workshop started," I said. "That was the last time I saw her, until... well, until this."

"I didn't see her at all," Quinn said. "I was talking with Peter, I guess."

"Who was she with?"

"Her husband," I said. "Nigel Melville. And before the workshop, I heard her talking with Alicia Fawkes, the head of the museum."

"Do you know what they were talking about?"

"The exhibits," I said. "They were having a difference of opinion on the direction Alicia was taking with the museum."

The deputy cocked an eyebrow. "Heated?"

"A little," I said.

"What did they say?"

I sighed. I'd talked to Alicia about the conversation, so even if I wanted to, I really couldn't lie and pretend I didn't know. "Priscilla didn't like that Alicia had brought this house to the property. She was going to make the board require Alicia to run everything by the board in the future, and I got the impression she was going to try to shut down this exhibit. Things were heated with her husband, too; she must have been having a bad night."

"How so?" Deputy Shames asked.

"They were arguing over money," I said. "It didn't sound like the marriage was going too well."

"It wasn't," Quinn said. "I heard he filed for divorce last week."

"What?" I asked.

"That's certainly interesting," the deputy said. "And you say he was here, too?"

"I think he only stayed for the first project," I said.

"Not the whole workshop?"

"I looked up at one point and he was gone. I think we were on the second recipe... it must have been about 30 minutes in that I noticed he was gone."

She took notes. "Did you see her talk with anyone else?"

"No," I said.

"And you didn't talk with her?"

"Nope," I said. "I've seen her, but we've never really intersected."

"Right," she said. She took a few more notes, then said, "You're free to go. Please let me know if you remember anything else."

"Where's Rooster?" Quinn asked.

"He's been spending more time at the office," she said after a brief pause that left me wondering. "Again, thank you, ladies, and please be in touch if you think of anything else."

Dismissed, Quinn and I walked to the front gate together. "Well, that was quite an evening," I said.

"I'd prefer a slightly less eventful one, myself," she said. "Poor Priscilla."

"I know," I said. What a horrible way to die... alone, locked into a room. I shuddered as I remembered her prone form at the door. What had happened to her? I wondered.

Are you really thinking of selling some of that balm Serafine taught us to make?" Quinn asked as we walked, both of us still shaken by what we had found.

"I am," I said. "I've been trying to come up with unique product ideas. I've already got soaps, lip balms, candles, so why not try selling healing balms and other skincare products?"

"Makes sense to me," she said. "I'm happy to carry some at the front of the Blue Onion Cafe if you'd like."

"That would be terrific," I said. "And you know if you ever get tired of running a stand, I'm happy to sell your baked goods, too."

"Well, if you start doing markets in Austin, that would be great. Peter's taken some pastries a few times, and they've done well." She sighed and glanced over her shoulder. "But I'm more worried about what's going on here. And then that voodoo doll in the tree..."

"Well, it's in the hands of the police now. Odds are good it had nothing to do with what happened today, anyway."

"I hope you're right," I said. As we approached the gate, I again caught a movement out of the corner of my eye. It was Arthur; he was leaning against a pillar in front of the blacksmith's forge, watching Quinn and me. As I caught his eye, he took a swig from a flask and melted back into the shadows. Something about him gave me the heebie-jeebies; if he was showing up to work drunk, I could see why Alicia wasn't thrilled to have him on the payroll. He was not a very attractive man; dark-haired, with a long, pudding-like face and a paunch, he was nothing at all like his glamorous sister. Priscilla's fortune was family money. Why was she running the board while he worked at a relatively menial job at one of her projects? I wondered. His last name was Graham, not Jordan... why the different surname? And had he learned of his sister's death? If so, he certainly didn't seem too torn up about it.

"Lucy?"

"What?" I turned; Quinn had been talking to me, and I hadn't heard a word. "Sorry," I said. "I saw Priscilla's brother by the blacksmith's forge. I got distracted."

"He's creepy," Quinn said in a low voice. "He walked over before the workshop started and all I could smell was that sour, stale alcohol smell. And he kept staring at me." She shivered. "He set off my spidey senses."

"How come he's just a menial while his sister's on the board?" I asked in a quiet voice as we closed the museum gate behind us.

"She's the family's golden child. He's a nephew her parents adopted when her aunt and uncle died."

"So all the money went to her." That explained what

Nigel said about Priscilla controlling her brother with money.

"Yup," Quinn said.

"That can't have been a happy family situation."

"You think he might have done her in?" Quinn asked.

"It's worth considering," I said. "Fortunately, Deputy Shames is on the case, so I'm feeling better than I would be if it was Rooster."

"What about Priscilla's son and his girlfriend?"

"They were here earlier, but I don't see them now... do you think someone's had a chance to tell the family yet?"

"Probably not yet. If her fortune goes to her son, Damian's girlfriend is going to be a very happy camper."

"What do you mean?"

"Apparently they're living together," Quinn told me. "And he got fired from his job as an intern at a law firm two days later. It seems they don't like it if you show up two hours late every day."

"That's interesting," I said. "Are you suggesting maybe he might have had something to do with what happened to Priscilla?"

"Assuming she didn't die of a heart attack or something, it's worth considering," she said. "Damian's girlfriend looks like she likes the finer things. A little family money would certainly make it easier to keep her in Kendra Scott jewelry, or whatever it is that's in style these days."

"We're putting the cart way before the horse here," I said. "We don't even know what happened to her."

"True," she said.

I sighed. "I don't know about you, but I'm ready to go home and leave all this behind me, though."

"Me too," she agreed.

A lot of things had creeped me out today, not least

finding Alicia dead in the Warren house. I was feeling in need of a good lavender bath and maybe a glass of wine. Too bad my boyfriend Tobias was out of town getting in hours to renew his vet certification, or I'd ask him to come over and keep me company.

Ah, well. That's what dogs are for, right?

5

***

The next morning was a bit warmer than I would have liked. As hard as it was to leave Chuck and the kittens in my cozy bed, I was glad I got up early to tackle my chores before the heat of the day. If early June was any indication, the rest of the summer was going to be a scorcher.

I fed everyone, did the milking, gathered eggs, and watered what was left of my garden, then grabbed a few baskets. I'd saved the best chore for last: picking peaches from the trees down by the creek. I loved being down in the orchard, listening to the burble of the water along the caliche creekbed--which would likely slow to a trickle within a few weeks--and the rustle of the morning breeze through the honey-scented sycamore trees. A few bits of "cotton" were floating in the air from the broad-leafed cottonwoods that dotted the creek banks, and I brushed some of the "summer snow" from the tip of my nose as I carried the ladder and baskets down to the orchard. The dewberries that grew by the water were about picked out for the year, the plants preparing to hunker down for the long, dry summer. The trees, thank-fully, were short enough that I only needed a small ladder to get to the top branches; within an hour, I had enough for a few batches of jam and some peach cobbler.

I made myself a quick lunch with some fresh mozzarella, one of the first tomatoes of the season, and a chunk of homemade bread with a smattering of fresh basil and some garlic salt. I wolfed it down, offering a few tidbits to Chuck and the kitties (who all liked bread, oddly), then cut up a peach and layered it over vanilla ice cream with a drizzle of honey.

My chores done and my stomach comfortably full, I grabbed a basket of peaches and got in my truck, leaving Chuck in charge of the kittens, a job he took very seriously. He was already keeping Lucky from digging up a philoden-dron plant when I closed the front door behind me and headed out to the truck.

It was a short drive to the Honeyed Moon Meadery, and not so warm I couldn't roll down the truck's windows. As I pulled into the meadery's courtyard, the smell of honey greeted me, along with the barking of several happy-looking dogs. Serafine ran an animal sanctuary, and there were always several dogs recovering from mange, broken legs, and maltreatment from former owners. Today, two golden retrievers, a pit mix, and a dog of indeterminate parentage barked and wagged at me as I parked and got out of the truck, peach basket in hand.

Serafine walked out of the barn as I closed the truck door, Chloe a few feet behind her. "I was hoping to see you today!" she said. "I put aside some beeswax for you when I got home."

"And I brought you some peaches," I said. "I'm planning

to make some jam later, but thought you might want some fresh ones."

"Ooh, wonderful. I love them on yogurt with some oats," she said. "I was just finishing bottling some mead; I'm a bit sticky." She wore a big white apron over a sparkly sleeveless dress, and it was spotted liberally with red liquid. Chloe, in overalls and a matching apron, also looked like she'd been in an abattoir rather than a meadery. "Looks like blood, doesn't it?" she grinned. "Smells better, though."

She was right; I caught a whiff of raspberry and honey on the breeze. "Berry mead?"

"Raspberry melomel," she said.

"That's right. Melomel." Melomel, I remembered, was fruit-flavored mead; she had taught me that a while back.

"I can finish up in there if you'd like," Chloe offered.

"That would be great," Serafine said, taking off her apron. "I've got to give Jelly Bean her medicine, anyway."

"Who's Jelly Bean?" I asked.

"The Chihuahua my neighbor found in the middle of the 955 the other day," Serafine told me. "We think someone dumped her. She's sweet as can be, but she's got tumors and probably a heart problem, according to the vet."

"Poor baby," I said as I followed her to the house she shared with her sister, Aimee.

"I know," she told me. "I don't understand how people can do things like that."

"Speaking of people doing things," I said, "did you hear about what happened to Priscilla?"

"No," she said. "I came home last night and crashed."

"She died in the Warren house," I said.

Serafine froze, one hand on the screen door handle, and turned to me. "What?"

"We found her last night," I said. "The police came out. It

wasn't Rooster, thankfully. I don't know if it was foul play, but they opened an investigation."

"Wow," Serafine said, opening the screen door and stepping into the house. "I knew Priscilla was unpopular, but I didn't know she was that unpopular."

"It's possible she could have died from natural causes, but she was relatively young," I said as I followed her into the house, which smelled of herbs, spices, beeswax... and Hoppin' John, a wonderful dish with black-eyed peas cooked long and slow with ham hocks and veggies. Aimee stood at the stove, her hair a curly halo around her head, stirring a big pot.

"Hey, Lucy? Staying for lunch? I'm about to whip up a batch of cornbread to go with these beans."

"It sounds delicious, but I've got a lot to do today," I said. "Thank you, though!"

"Remember that chairwoman I told you about?" Serafine said to her sister.

"The one who didn't want you teaching grandma's salves?"

"That's the one," Serafine said with a grimace. "She's dead."

Aimee put down her wooden spoon. "What? How?"

"We don't know yet," I said. "Quinn and I found her locked into the Warren house. She looked like she was trying to get out, but the door was latched from the outside."

"That's horrible!" Aimee said.

"How well did you know Priscilla?" I asked Serafine as she reached down to retrieve a very small, very old looking Chihuahua from a round, fluffy bed.

"Sweet Jelly Bean," Serafine cooed. The little dog blinked large brown eyes and then licked Serafine on the chin before she could answer my question. "We chatted a few times in the office," she told me, stroking the little dog's gray ears. "But that would hardly be enough to put me in her enemy column."

"Was it a long column?" I asked.

"Long enough," Serafine said as she retrieved a medicine bottle and slid out a pill.

"Who else was on it?"

Serafine dug through the pantry, emerged with a jar of peanut butter, and took out a dollop on a spoon. She nestled the pill into it and offered it to Jelly Bean, who lapped it up with a long, pink tongue. "I was talking with her husband, Nigel, the other day. Apparently they weren't all one big happy family."

"Quinn told me he had filed for divorce," I said.

Serafine dropped the spoon and looked up sharply. "What?"

"I told you," Aimee said from the kitchen. "He's got it bad," she continued. "Don't need the cards to tell me that."

"What do you mean?" I asked.

"Nigel Melville has been in love with Serafine since they volunteered together at the museum six months ago," Aimee said.

"He isn't in love with me," Serafine scoffed.

Aimee rolled her eyes. "Uh huh."

"Did Priscilla know about it?"

"She didn't just fall off the turnip truck," Aimee said. "Of course she knew. Anyone who saw them spend more then ten seconds together knew."

That explained the look exchanged between them at the workshop... and possibly why Nigel was attending the workshop in the first place.

Serafine bent and picked up her spoon, placing it on the counter, and then continued to stroke Jelly Bean's soft ears.

"I'm not saying he's in love with me, but we do... well, we do get along. But I don't mess with married men, and I told him as much."

"Which is why he filed for divorce, I'm guessing," Aimee said.

Serafine's eyes flashed. "Don't put that on me."

"It's not on you," Aimee said. "It was his choice."

"Well, no wonder Priscilla wasn't crazy about you teaching that class."

"Oh, that's not the only reason," Serafine said. "I represent a part of history she'd rather not see every time she goes to the museum."

"Did you tell Lucy about our DNA results?" Aimee asked.

"She did," I said.

"So you heard we've got kin in the area," Aimee said, her eyes sparkling.

"I know! And I thought your whole family was from Louisiana!"

"So did we," Serafine said, "but we found three cousins just outside of LaGrange."

"That really is great news," I said. "But how did that happen?"

"We don't know," she said. "We've been trying to figure it out. There seems to be a missing link somewhere."

"Like maybe somebody was sowin' their wild oats a bit," Aimee said.

Serafine glanced at her sister. "It's... well, a little bit awkward, actually. Like I told you, we've been e-mailing, and we're supposed to meet this week."

"That's so exciting," I said. "I hope you figure out the mystery of what happened."

"It's a mystery for sure," Serafine agreed. "Their folks

didn't travel much, from what they've told me by email, leastways not to Louisiana. We aren't sure yet exactly how we're related, and none of us can figure out what the heck happened."

"Maybe you can piece it together through birth records?"

"I don't have birth certificates for anyone other than my parents," Serafine said. "Maybe they'll have something to go on."

"I hope so," I said.

"Me too, but we've got bigger fish to fry," Aimee said. "If that Priscilla woman's gone, does that mean the Warren house exhibit is a go?"

"I hope so," Serafine said. "I guess it depends on who takes her place on the board."

"Maybe Flora Kocurek will step up; she'd be on our side, I'm sure." I knew Flora was on the board, and since I'd helped her find out who'd killed her mother a few years back, we'd become friends. "Back to what you were saying about the Jordan clan being a not-so-happy family," I said. "You were talking about Nigel, right?"

"Actually, I was talking about her son, Damian. He hasn't been having much luck getting into law school, and he just lost his job. I think he was expecting his mother to bankroll him. I heard a rumor that she was going to cut him off if he didn't get into school or find gainful employment."

"Sounds reasonable," I said. "What do you know about Priscilla's brother?"

"I know he wasn't thrilled to be working at the museum," Serafine said. "And he wasn't overly fond of his sister."

"What's up with that, anyway?"

"I heard a rumor that because he was adopted, he wasn't in the will."

"I heard that, too."

"He's actually Priscilla's cousin. Her mother's sister passed, so the family took him on. Because Arthur wasn't one of his biological kids, though, Daddy decided he wasn't supposed to inherit anything."

"That's what I heard, too. So his sister controlled the purse strings."

"He could have gone and gotten a job," Aimee pointed out. "Nobody was stoppin' him from making a life for himself."

"That's certainly true," I said. "But it must be hard to have a sibling who's left everything, when you have nothing. It can't feel good. Like you're not really part of the family."

"Money can be the devil, can't it?" Serafine said, shaking her head.

"Thank goodness that's one problem we don't have to deal with," Aimee said playfully, but there was an edge to the jest.

"Everything okay?" I asked.

"It's been a little bit tight lately," Serafine admitted. "We lost some accounts; that's part of the reason we're trying to expand the business. And where are my manners... can I get you something to drink?"

"I'd love that," I said. "Do you have any of that honey tea around?"

"Of course!" Aimee said, fishing a bottle out of the refrigerator. "You like it?"

"I love it," I said as I took the lid off and sipped some of the refreshing brew. "Who came up with this?"

"We both did," Serafine said.

"I think you've got a winner on your hands," I told them. I took another sip and was about to broach the topic of the doll I'd found by the Warren house--and the one I'd spotted on my own property--when Chloe popped through the front door.

"Smells good in here," she said.

"Lunch in about half an hour," Aimee informed her.

"That's one of the best parts of working here: the food," Chloe said.

"Lucy brought some news," Serafine told her.

Chloe turned her big eyes to me. "Oh? What is it?"

"Priscilla Jordan-Melville is dead," I said.

Chloe blinked. "What? How?"

"I don't know. Quinn and I found her in the Warren house at the museum."

"Poor Nigel," she said. She was hugging herself, but based on the excitement I saw glinting in her eyes, she didn't look too mournful at the news. "He must be just heartbroken."

"You know they were getting a divorce, right?"

"What?" she asked, in a tinny voice that sounded well, unbelievable. "I had no idea." Her head swiveled to Serafine. "Does that mean you two will start dating now?"

Aimee put down the bag of cornmeal she'd pulled out of the pantry. "Chloe!"

"What?" The young woman blinked again, all innocence. "Everyone knows you two are sweet on each other."

"That's enough," Serafine said in a flat voice. "Why don't you go wash up, and we'll see you back when lunch is ready."

Chloe's pale face flushed under her sparkly makeup, and she shot Serafine a sullen look before heading back outside.

"What was that all about?" I asked when the door shut behind her.

"She doesn't always have the best filter," Aimee said. "We're working on sanding down the rough edges."

"How did you find her, anyway?"

"I put an ad in for an assistant when things were good," Serafine said. "We hired her a few months ago. She's been a good worker, and I hate to let her go."

"She kind of views Serafine as a goddess, although I have no idea why," Aimee said, rolling her eyes. "I caught her trying on one of Serafine's dresses in the mirror the other day."

"I'm her mentor," Serafine explained. "She doesn't have a lot of family she's close to; I think she's just hungry for a mother figure."

"Maybe. I think she'd wear your skin if she could, Ser," Aimee said.

I took another sip of my tea. "Sounds like she's got some boundary issues."

"You think?" Serafine said with a wry smile, then took a sip from her own bottle of tea. "She's got a good heart, though, and we all have our struggles."

"That she does," Aimee agreed. "She's got good people instincts, too; although it's not hard to figure out that Nigel's sweet on you."

"Nonsense," Serafine said, but she didn't meet her sister's eye.

"And I'd say it's mutual," Aimee continued.

"Enough," Serafine said. "He's a nice man, but his wife just died. Let's not start with the matchmaking, okay?"

6

"*W*hatever you say." As Aimee cracked eggs into a bowl for the cornbread, I looked around the little house the Alexandres called home. Beeswax candles joined the scent of Aimee's Hoppin' John in perfuming the space, bundles of herbs hung from a beam in the kitchen-- doubtless medicinal plants to be used for infusions and balms--and a basket of cloth remnants lay on the coffee table. My eyes were caught by a scrap of red fabric near the top of the pile that looked familiar.

"What's this for?" I asked, picking up the basket.

"Oh, we use that for making sachets or patching things," Serafine said. "We try to re-use everything around here."

"My grandmother kept a scrap basket, too." As I sorted through the fabric, I palmed the scrap of red fabric and tucked it into my pocket. I didn't like doing it, but I had to know if it matched the fabric on the doll at my farm. "I really enjoyed the salve-making. Your grandmother taught you a lot of things, didn't she?"

"She did. She did a lot of healing, especially with plants.

But a lot of people didn't go to her because she wouldn't work with both hands."

"Work with both hands?" I asked. "What does that mean?"

"A lot of folks believe that rootwork isn't all about doing positive things. That curses and the dark side of the work have their place in creating balance in the world. Like, if you had an abusive spouse and there was no other way to get rid of him, a curse was okay."

"But not your grandmother."

"No," she confirmed. "That wasn't her way; she wouldn't meddle with love spells or jinxes or any of that. She wanted to be a healer, and she was good at it."

"So... no voodoo dolls, or anything like that?" I asked.

"She called them doll babies. I only remember her making one a few times, like if someone's aunt had cancer or some other ailment and wanted her help but wasn't in town, she'd pray over the doll baby instead of the person. She always got consent, though. Always."

"Do you ever use them?" I asked.

"No," she said, shaking her head. "I pretty much stick to plants and business," she told me, with a grin. "Aimee is a little more into the spirit side than I am... she does readings, and we both have a little bit of the sight."

"Nothing like that Teena Marburger, though," Aimee said. "She's scary good." Teena, a young woman in town, was well known for her knack for "seeing" things.

"She is, isn't she?" I asked. "Anyone else in town make doll babies that you know of?" I asked.

"No," Serafine said, and her brow crinkled. "Why?"

Before I could answer, there was a knock at the door.

"I'll get it," Serafine said.

She walked over and opened the door. I couldn't see

who was there, but I could hear him. "You're not answering my calls or my texts. Why?"

"I'm so sorry about your wife. It's terrible, I know, but... I just can't do this right now. This just isn't the time," she said. "I'll be in touch soon, I promise."

"But Serafine..."

"Not now," she said. "I'm sorry. I'll call you soon, I promise. She closed the door firmly and locked it, then turned around, eyes wide, looking rattled.

"Told you he was sweet on you," Aimee said.

"Nigel?" I asked.

"Yeah," Serafine admitted. "I'll admit he's attractive, but he's too... insistent. And his wife just passed yesterday, and he's at my doorstep today. It's creepy."

"It is," Aimee said, shivering.

I glanced over at the basket. "Has he been here before?"

"He's come for a couple of readings from me," Aimee said. "But he really just wanted to see Serafine."

"Where do you do the readings?"

"Kitchen table, mostly," she said as she stirred milk into the cornbread batter and poured it into a pan.

"What did they say?"

"Oh, typical for someone in a troubled marriage, I'd say. Three of swords, seven of swords. Lots of swords, really. Tower Card."

"What does that mean?"

"I shouldn't say, really. Basically, heartbreak. Betrayal. Upheaval."

"Betrayal? By whom?"

Aimee and Serafine exchanged glances. "I shouldn't say more," Aimee said, tucking the pan of cornbread into the oven.

I LEFT a half hour later with a few blocks of beeswax, along with more salve recipes than I knew what to do with. I was getting excited about the prospect of adding a new line to my market wares... but nervous about the scrap of fabric in my pocket.

I got home and let Chuck out for a potty break, then stored the beeswax and recipes in the pantry and went outside to retrieve what I now knew to be a doll baby from the smokehouse. I took the piece of fabric from my pocket and compared it to the fabric on the little beeswax figurine.

It was a match, right down to the frayed edge.

"WHAT'S WRONG?" Tobias asked when he swung by just after seven, with a to-go pack of Rosita's enchiladas and a big bag of chips. He'd gotten back from his continuing education classes that afternoon, and had offered to bring dinner.

"What's not wrong?" I asked as he put down the bags and pulled me into a big hug.

"Still upset over finding Priscilla?" he asked as Chuck gamboled around our feet.

"Yeah," I said. "And a few other things."

"Like what?" he asked. Smudge began climbing his jeans leg; he released me, reached down and scooped the kitten up with one hand, then with the other petted Chuck, who rolled over to offer his belly.

"I think Serafine left a doll baby--a voodoo doll--on my fence when she was here. And I saw another one outside the house where we found Priscilla."

"Did you talk to Serafine about it?"

I grimaced. "I asked if she worked with dolls, and she said no. But I found this fabric in her scrap basket, and it matches what was on the doll I found on my fence." I showed him what I had discovered; he held the little figurine as if it were going to explode in his hand, then put it down quickly. "I found it--and the goats and cattle out--right after she left the other day, when she was looking at my hives."

"Why would she leave something like that on your fence?"

"I don't know," I said. "How am I supposed to ask something like that? And when I was over there, Priscilla's husband Nigel came to see her. Serafine sent him away, but..."

"You think she might have something to do with what happened to Priscilla? That maybe Serafine and Nigel were involved?"

"I don't know," I said. "If I trusted the police more, I'd talk to them, but with Rooster as sheriff, I'm afraid they'd just lock her up and not look any further. I don't know what to do."

"Well, first, let's find out why she died," Tobias said, pushing a strand of hair out of my face. "And in the meantime, let's pop open a couple of beers and have some enchiladas. I'm sorry I don't have margaritas, but they don't sell them to go."

"I've got tequila," I offered.

"Let's start with Shiner," he suggested, and together we set the Mexican food up on my kitchen table. He spent the next hour or so filling me in on the day's travails, which included a cow with a displaced uterus, a goat who had gotten caught in barbed wire, and a standard poodle who had eaten a package of light bulbs and needed emergency surgery.

"Will the dog be okay?" I asked.

"I'm hoping so," I said. "Rebecca is monitoring her down at the clinic; she'll call if anything changes, and I'll check in on her on the way home."

"I hope she'll be all right," I said.

"How's your clan?" he asked.

"I've still got to go milk everyone and do my evening chores," I said, "but everyone was accounted for when I got home a little while ago."

"I'll give you a hand if you like."

"You've had a tough day already; why don't you just relax? I'll make us a peach cobbler when I'm done; I picked peaches today."

"In that case, I'm definitely helping. The sooner you get your chores done, the sooner we get to eat cobbler!"

MANY HANDS DO MAKE light work; with Tobias's expert help, I was done in no time at all, and we were back in the kitchen peeling peaches side by side. I was making Texas Peach Cobbler, which involved a cakey, buttery topping over a bed of sweetened peaches; it was perfect with a scoop of vanilla ice cream, which (of course) I had in the freezer.

Tobias and I had just put the last of the sliced, peeled peaches in the bottom of the pan when the phone rang. It was Aimee.

"Did you hear?" she asked.

"No. What?"

"They arrested Serafine a half hour ago. For murder."

7

"*T*hat doesn't make any sense at all," I said. "Why would Serafine kill Priscilla? Of all the people I can think of, she had the least reason to want to kill her."

"They say she was actually involved with Nigel, and that she wanted Priscilla out of the way so she could marry Nigel and get all of the Jordans' money, so she gave him a bottle of tea laced with strychnine to poison her with."

Well, that explained the bitter taste on her lips when I administered CPR. "All right, I know Serafine is attracted to Nigel, but Serafine told me they weren't involved."

"They texted some, but no more than that."

So there was some concrete evidence of a connection. But that still didn't make Serafine a murderer.

"Serafine's smarter than to give Priscilla a poisoned bottle of her own labeled tea," I said. "Is that what they used as evidence?"

"They found a doll baby outside the Warren house," Aimee said. "Even though Serafine doesn't practice voodoo, they think she put it there as some kind of... token, or something. I don't know. Why were you asking about that, anyway?"

"I don't know," I lied. "Just curious, I guess. Anyway, I can think of about a half a dozen other people with more motive than Serafine. Like Nigel. And the museum director. Or even Priscilla's brother, or her son."

"You think Alicia might have killed her over the Warren house?"

"She was pretty angry the other night," I said. "I'm not saying it's her. I'm just saying the police haven't cast a very wide net, is all."

"Can you help her?" Aimee said. "Like you did before?"

I sighed. "I'll try," I said. "But are you sure Serafine wasn't making doll babies?"

"She's never made one that I know of," Aimee said. "And I know she didn't kill Priscilla Jordan-Melville."

"I'm so sorry this happened," I said. "Do you have someone staying with you?"

"Chloe's here," she said. "She... she just made a pot of tea for me. I'll be okay. Just... help me get my sister out of jail, okay?"

"I'll do whatever I can," I promised. "Can I bring dinner tomorrow?"

"Sure," Aimee said, sounding more disheartened than I'd ever heard her. "But more than anything, I need my sister back."

"I'll do everything I can," I promised, and we hung up a moment later.

Tobias was watching me. "So it was murder."

"Apparently it was," I said. "There was strychnine in her tea. And Serafine's in jail for it."

"And you promised Aimee you'll try to get her out?"

"What else was I supposed to do?" I asked, slumping

down into one of the kitchen chairs. "I can't believe Serafine would kill Priscilla. Why would she? I think the police are just being lazy."

"Did they suggest a motive?"

"According to Aimee, the police say she was involved with Nigel, and killed Priscilla so that they could be together and she'd have access to Priscilla's money to save her business. She mentioned today that things weren't as good as they had been; I know Honeyed Moon recently lost some accounts, but Serafine was working to diversify with the tea business."

"Is Nigel a suspect?"

"I don't know," I said. "He was there that night, and he and Priscilla did argue." I cast my mind back to that night. "He disappeared part of the way through the workshop, now that I think of it. Maybe he went and found Priscilla and spiked her drink. Someone locked her into that house."

"Strychnine works fast," Tobias said.

"Then why lock her in somewhere?"

"So she couldn't get help? So she wouldn't attract attention?"

I shuddered.

"Nigel had opportunity, and as for motive... he might have been in a better financial position if she died than if they divorced," Tobias pointed out. "It's possible she had some knowledge that would damage him if it came out in court."

"That's true. And he did show up at Serafine's today."

"Maybe he was obsessed with Serafine and sent her some texts that Priscilla saw. So he got her out of the way so he could be with Serafine?"

"They were already divorcing," I said. "Why bother?"

"Money?" he suggested. "You mentioned the director of the museum had issues with her, too."

"She was being railroaded by Priscilla," I said. "Priscilla was trying to control all the decisions... including putting the kibosh on the Warren house exhibit. Plus, she had to give Priscilla's brother a job, even though he made her uncomfortable." I sat up. "He's a possibility, too. I mean, his sister is rolling in it, and he's got a pity job at the museum. He was there that night. Maybe she made him mad."

"Strychnine indicates planning," Tobias pointed out. "And somebody had to have the opportunity to slip it into her tea."

I groaned. "I think it may be time for tequila."

"In the pie safe?" he asked.

"Top shelf," I said. "Let's get this cobbler going and sit out on the porch. I need some fresh air."

I slid the cobbler into the oven and set the timer as Tobias poured us two shots of tequila and cut up a lime from the bowl on the counter.

Together, we walked out onto the front porch. "Serafine was going to help me with my hives," I said.

"What's wrong with them?"

"They need new queens," I said. "And without Serafine's help..." It was hard to imagine life in Buttercup without Serafine's generous, wise presence. "How am I going to figure out what happened to Priscilla?"

"Start with the family, I'd say."

I sighed. "Looks like time to bake cookies and make some consolation house calls."

"And hang out at the museum a little more, too."

"It's a busy season here, though," I said.

"I'll help out if you need it," he volunteered. "And I'll be at the museum, too; I take care of the livestock, remember? I can poke around."

"But your practice..."

"If Serafine's innocent, she shouldn't be in jail. If we can help her, I'm in." He looked at me. "Are you sure she's innocent?"

I wanted to say yes immediately, but I kept thinking of that doll baby on the fence. A rush of guilt flooded me that I wasn't sure. "I think she's innocent," I said firmly. "And somebody's got to do a proper investigation."

"Well, if the police can't figure it out, I'm sure you can," Tobias said.

"I hope you're right." I said.

As SOON AS my chores were done the next morning, I checked the fences--Hot Lips had been looking restless lately, and I was worried she might make another break for it--then high-tailed it over to the Heritage Museum, hoping to get a chance to talk to anyone who might be able to shed light on what had happened to Priscilla.

Tobias and I had stayed up till way past our bedtimes, sitting in rocking chairs on the porch, watching the stars, petting kittens, and discussing everything under the sun.

Now, with a cottage cheese kolache from the Blue Onion cafe in my hand (I'd stopped by to say hi to Quinn), I was walking into the Heritage Museum, enjoying the breeze off the rolling hills surrounding the little compound of antique houses and barns and trying not to think too hard about what I'd found in the Warren house the day before.

"Lucy!" Alicia looked up from her cluttered desk as I stepped into the main office. "How are you doing?"

"As well as can be expected," I told her.

"Horrible thing yesterday," she said, clutching the abalone pendant she often wore. She'd told me once that she'd found the piece as a child in what turned out to be a Native American archeological site; it had been her North Star, so to speak, ever since. "I'm so sorry you had to be the one who found her. And I'm so upset that there's more bad press associated with the Warren house."

She didn't seem terribly broken up about Priscilla's death, I noticed. "What do you mean?"

"Mandy Vargas down at the *Buttercup Zephyr* has been doing some research for me into the archives so we can put together the history of the house; she's writing a story on the grand opening. It turns out that one of the former residents is a man who disappeared. He had just been acquitted of a minor robbery two days before he vanished." She shook her head. "Mandy thinks he was murdered."

8

"*M*urdered?" I repeated. This must be the story Quinn heard at the café.

"There was a lot of... well, let's call it 'vigilante justice' back then. The crime was widely considered to be trumped up charges--normally nothing to get too riled up about--but apparently the sheriff's daughter was sweet on this man Garland, and the sheriff didn't like that much."

"A Kocurek?" I'd been told that our current sheriff, Rooster Kocurek, was just the latest in a long line of Kocurek sheriffs.

She nodded. "Mandy thinks that he was given a second, unofficial trial... and that he didn't make it out alive. It happened sometimes like that, unfortunately."

"That's awful," I said. "In other words, he was killed just because the sheriff's daughter had a crush on him?"

"That's what Mandy thinks. She hasn't found any evidence yet, except for an interview with a man named Ezra Bilton, who's 95 years old. He was Garland's best friend."

"I can't imagine something like that happening," I breathed.

"The family left soon after; they said it was a bad-luck house." She grimaced. "I don't believe much in the supernatural, but to have Priscilla die there just before the grand opening... it makes you wonder."

"You know they arrested Serafine?"

"I heard," she told me, frowning. "And that she was supposed to have poisoned Priscilla with some tea. I think it's ridiculous. Just because Serafine argued with her doesn't mean she killed her."

"What do you mean, argued?"

"Priscilla told Serafine she didn't want her 'peddling her voodoo cures' here. Serafine took offense, to put it mildly." Serafine hadn't mentioned that, I thought to myself. "On top of it, Priscilla found some little doll hanging outside her house the other day, too. She was sure it was Serafine who left it there."

"What did it look like?" I asked, thinking of the two I had already found.

"Some kind of wax thing wrapped up in cloth. I heard her accuse Serafine of leaving it there."

"What did she do with it?"

"The doll?" Alicia shrugged. "I don't know. I wouldn't be surprised if she was making it up. Anyway, I had to tell the police what I had heard, of course, and I'm guessing they figured Serafine decided Priscilla was a problem and wanted to get rid of her. Priscilla didn't have the tea bottle on her when I saw her, though, but I'm guessing Serafine could have given her one."

"If Serafine was mad at her, why would she give her a bottle of tea?"

"To poison her, of course."

"Why would Serafine even have wanted to poison Priscilla?" I asked.

"Anger, I suppose," she told me. "Serafine felt Priscilla was trying to... well, whitewash history, so to speak. They had it out a few days ago, too, when Priscilla told her she should focus her talk on more European-based remedies. Serafine refused, and I defended her by trying to explain it to Priscilla."

"What did you tell her?"

"I told her that the salves Serafine was teaching about were often used in Buttercup back in the day... and almost certainly by some of the people living in the houses at the museum. Heck... most of the buildings here were built by enslaved people, and they almost certainly used remedies that had been passed down through the generations."

"I didn't know the buildings weren't built by the owners."

"Well, one of them was," she said. "The Krueger house was built by the family who lived in it. But the other two families, the Jordans and the Balls, used the labor of enslaved people to build their homes and take care of their farms. All the more reason to include multiculturally sourced recipes in our workshops. Besides, it turns out Serafine's from here; did you hear about her genetic testing results?"

"I did," I said. "She told me she's got kin in the area."

"Isn't it exciting?" Alicia lit up for a moment, then remembered where Serafine was. "I just hope she gets to meet them. She has no idea how they're related, but it's a whole branch. It's like someone just transplanted a couple of generations back and cut all ties."

"I wonder why?"

"It's a mystery," she said. "One I hope we'll have a chance to dig into."

"Well, we'll just have to figure out who really killed Priscilla," I said, watching Alicia's face. Her smile wobbled a bit, but then she was right back on track.

"It's really thrown the board into a tizzy," she said. "I've been ordered to put a hold on everything until we've got things back in order; there's an emergency meeting to elect a new chair soon."

"Oh? I know Flora Kocurek's on the board; who else is?'

"Nigel, and Edna Mueller."

Edna and Flora were big rollers in town, I knew. I'd have to track down Flora and find out if she had any info on the situation.

"Any of them have an eye on the chair position?"

"Are you seriously suggesting that someone might have killed Priscilla just so they could be chair of the board? You do realize it's not a paying position?"

"So maybe it's crazy. I just thought... I kind of got the feeling Priscilla might have been at odds with other board members as to the direction of the museum."

"Well, she did want to gloss over some of the less pleasant chapters of Buttercup's history, I'll give you that," she said. "I think she really envisioned this place as a testament to the Jordan family rather than a history of Buttercup."

"Why?"

"Her ancestors came from Tennessee and started a cotton-farming operation back in the 1800s. And with her donating the 100 acres of land and the original farm house, she feels... well, ownership of the place, even though it's not her family's anymore."

"Was the rest of the board in line with her?"

"She was leading the charge. It's no secret that her husband was dead-set against her. If anything, he's probably the most likely candidate for killing her. They were divorcing, you know."

"I heard," I said. "Was it contentious?"

"She was going to hire the toughest lawyer in Houston, from what I hear," she said. "She wanted it all."

"Sounds like her family is used to having it all," I commented.

"I think you're right," she agreed with a sigh. "Except her brother, anyway – and he's adopted."

"I heard about that. That's got to have been hard to grow up with," I said. "Feeling like a second-class citizen."

"I don't think that changed. Now, she keeps—kept--him on a leash with an allowance. But she still made me give him work here. Total nepotism."

"I've heard that. He can't fend for himself?"

"I don't know if he's ever tried, and he's certainly no use to me here either," she said. "Although I can understand why he's like this, even if I wish I was rid of him. It's got to be miserable to be passed over like that, when there's just so much money."

"How much money are we talking?"

"Millions," she said. "Plus she still owns almost 3,000 acres of land."

"And none of it went to him."

"Apparently, everything was put into a trust that all went to her," she said. "Every penny. I think it was understood that she would 'take care of' her brother."

"That's not an approach geared toward family harmony, is it?"

She laughed. "Oh, the first rule of the Jordan family was to protect the family money. Everything and everyone who wasn't part of the direct genetic line was secondary." She snorted. "It's no wonder her marriage was falling apart."

"Hard to be with someone when you're not really on the same team, I guess. Still... I kind of got the impression her husband was looking elsewhere a bit, maybe?"

"You mean Serafine?" She sighed. "I'm pretty sure he has a major crush on her. But I'm also pretty sure she held the line with him."

"So you think she likes him, too?"

"What's not to like?" Alicia asked. "He's handsome, articulate, witty..."

"And married."

"Not anymore," she pointed out with a raised eyebrow.

"I hear the police have some evidence of their connection," I said.

"Well, it's not a relationship. They're just friends."

"Still. Not good for Serafine."

"No. I still don't understand when exactly they think she poisoned her," she said.

"Me neither," I said. "She was at the workshop the whole time. And I saw Priscilla at the beginning of the workshop; she didn't have a bottle of tea then."

"Unless she put it down outside somewhere. Or picked one up on the way out. Even so, when would Serafine have had a chance to poison it? She was in front of the room the whole time."

Or lock her into the Warren house, I thought to myself. "You might want to mention that to the police if you get a chance," I suggested.

"You think?"

"If Serafine didn't do it, it's not fair for her to go to jail for it."

"The question is," the director asked, "if Serafine didn't do it, who did?"

"Who would you put your money on?" I asked.

"I hate to say it," she said, pursing her lips, "but probably Nigel."

"Why?"

She shrugged. "No love lost between those two lately. Easier to settle an estate than fight for it in court."

"I thought all the money was in a trust. Who gets it?"

"That's an interesting question, isn't it?" she asked. "My money, so to speak, is on her son. But I guess we'll find out soon enough."

WHEN I LEFT THE OFFICE, I walked across the meadow toward the barn where last night's workshop had been held. The galvanized tub that had held Serafine's bottled teas still stood near the barn door. I stopped to examine it. The remaining bottles had been removed, whether by the museum director or the police I didn't know, and all that remained was a little bit of water... and a fragment of a torn label, which had dried and stuck to the metal. I peeled the label off the side of the tub. It wasn't from one of Serafine's tea bottles. It was a piece of an Arizona Tea label, which was strange, really. I hadn't seen anyone drinking Arizona Tea.

I tucked the label fragment into my pocket and walked into the barn, wondering if maybe the label was from a previous event. The tables were still in the same arrangement they had been last night. I walked around the big dusty space, stepping on the bits of hay scattered on the wood floor. Dust motes swirled in the sunlight that streamed in through the high windows. I could still smell a hint of the herbs Serafine had used yesterday, along with a whiff of beeswax and the clean scent of hay, mixed with the must of old wood.

How had Priscilla gotten her hands on a poisoned bottle of tea? Had someone handed it to her? Or had she taken it from the tub and just gotten unlucky?

Something told me that Priscilla's death wasn't a result of a strychnine-based game of Russian roulette. Someone had either given her a poisoned bottle or introduced the strychnine after she'd opened it. I tried to remember if I'd seen her with a bottle of tea in her hand when she was talking with Alicia... or if she'd had one with her during her altercation with her soon-to-be-ex-husband Nigel.

I walked out of the barn and headed back toward the little house where I'd found Priscilla's body. The crime scene tape hadn't been up very long. It was already gone; just a small fragment fluttered in the breeze, dangling from one of the oak trees by the front corner of the house. I pushed open the door and stepped inside, shivering at the memory of what I'd found yesterday and making sure to leave the door wide open behind me; I didn't want to be trapped in here like Priscilla had.

There was nothing in the room I hadn't seen the day before; light leaked through the small windows--windows too small to fit through, making it a perfect room to keep someone from getting out to get help. The only change I could see was the absence of Priscilla's body. As I stepped back out and closed the door behind me, I examined the latch. It moved easily, but you had to lean against the door to make it fall into place. Which confirmed my suspicion: someone had intentionally locked her in.

As I pulled the door and slid the latch into place, a rustle in the leaves behind me caught my attention. I whirled around and caught a flash of movement in the undergrowth.

"Hello?" I called. Silence, and then another crunch of

leaves. Footsteps, receding into the dark tangle of shrubs leading down to the creek.

Goose bumps rose on my arms, and I looked back at the little house where Priscilla had died.

Had her murderer just been spying on me?

And if so, why?

9

I walked toward the Jordan House and the veggie garden next to it, still spooked by the idea of someone watching me, and thinking about the history of this place. Of the three families who owned the houses originally at the museum, the Jordans had been the wealthiest of the bunch, with a house that must have been considered a mansion at the time, complete with outbuildings and a huge garden.

I kept an eye on my surroundings as I walked, but saw no sign of anything but birds and squirrels. I didn't have a lot of time to spend weeding, but I did want to check the water situation; unlike at the farm, any watering here had to be done by hand, using the pump near the back porch of the house. As I approached the yellow house with its white picket fence, I reflected that I'd never known it was built with unpaid labor. I'd envisioned the original inhabitants constructing the pier-and-beam structure by themselves, but evidently that hadn't been what had happened. The kitchen was a ways behind the house, as a fire preventative; Alicia had told me that next to childbirth, fire was the primary killer of women, whose large skirts were prone to accidentally brushing the flames and catching. I wondered where had the enslaved workers had lived. The smoke-house, outhouse, animal barn, low-slung kitchen/weaving room complex and main barn had survived the ravages of time, but there was no sign of servant or slave quarters. Had the workers lived where they labored, in the kitchen?

As I opened the little gate that led to the large vegetable garden, I thought of the hands that had opened that gate before mine. Who had tended this plot of land, now green with lush tomato plants, sprawling cucumbers, okra, and a little corner of herbs? I had planted rosemary, thyme, sage, dill, and Mexican mint marigold... Serafine had gathered the calendula flowers for making oils to soothe the skin, and the plants were now wilted and brown in the early summer heat. I made a mental note to replace them with some young basil plants; it was late in the season, but extra watering should pull them through.

I pumped a few buckets and filled the ollas in the tomato beds—narrow-necked unglazed terra cotta pots that we'd buried in the ground with their necks and mouths exposed, an ancient method used to water garden plants and minimize water loss. Then I did a quick search for squash vine borers, which had invaded my own crookneck squash patch the week before. I spotted one culprit near the end of the row, and headed to the shed to retrieve a knife. Squash vine borer moths laid eggs at the base of the stem; for the young larvae the remedy was to slice open the stem and kill the larva before it could kill the young plant. Not my favorite farm chore, but better than dustbusting squash bugs. (Handy tip? Empty the dustbuster before stowing it in your laundry room.)

The garden shed door was ajar when I got there, which

wasn't unusual--I wasn't the only person taking care of the garden, after all. Although the shed was usually quite orga-nized, today, the knife we used for borers wasn't hanging where it usually hung on the wall. In fact, the whole shed seemed in disarray. A bag of worm castings lay on the shed floor, and next to the castile soap, the cardboard can of Sluggo lay on its side, the granules scattered on the shelf. As I righted it, I spotted a brown plastic jug I didn't recognize. I picked it up; the label was half-torn off, but I spotted the word DANGER, in red, at the bottom of it. The top bore an oval logo that said "Martin's" above what appeared to be a picture of a brown, smooth-furred animal and the letters "Go." Below it were the letters STRY, in green.

"Oh," I said involuntarily, and set it down as if it were poison.

Because it was.

I HURRIED out of the shed, abandoning my gardening duties, and headed directly to the office, where Alicia was busy staring at her computer screen.

Alicia lowered her reading glasses when I walked in. "What's wrong?" she asked.

"I think I found the poison."

"Poison? What poison?"

"Strychnine," I said.

"Oh." She paled. "Where?"

"In the garden shed. I think it's gopher bait."

"But the gardens are organic!" she said.

"I know. And we don't have a gopher problem."

She leaned back in her chair, looking confused. "Then why is there gopher poison in the shed?"

"I'm guessing someone wants to make it look as if somebody who tends the garden was responsible for poisoning Priscilla's tea."

"That's crazy! The only people who tend the garden are you, Peter, me..." Her eyes widened. "And Serafine."

"She only dabbles in the herb garden," I pointed out. "Anyone could have gotten in there, though; we don't keep the shed locked. We don't generally keep dangerous chemicals."

"Yes, but..." She sighed and reached for the phone. "You know I have to report this. It really doesn't look good for Serafine, does it?"

"Of course," I said, then fixed her with a look. "Just make sure whoever you talks to knows that anyone could have gotten into the shed. And lots of people make visits to Heritage Farms."

"I'll tell them," she said, and as she dialed, I glanced down at the desk. A stack of bills lay in a folder on the corner of the desk: the top one, for the electric bill, was marked PAST DUE. Beneath it, peeking out, was a VISA bill; the balance listed was eye-popping. The top transaction was for almost eight hundred dollars. Alicia saw me looking and flipped the folder shut with her free hand, tucking it into a drawer. "Thanks for coming by," she mouthed, and a moment later, as I turned and walked out of the office, I heard her say, "Hello? This is Alicia Fawkes, from Jordan Heritage Farm? I'd like to make a report..."

I sighed as I closed the office door behind me. I didn't know what the normal financial status of non-profit organizations was, but things weren't looking too good for Heritage Farms.

Had Alicia been hiding the organization's financial situation... or possibly using the non-profit's credit card for her own uses?

And was it possible she'd killed Priscilla before she could expose her?

$\mathcal{T}$he sun was low in the sky later that day when I got to the Honeyed Moon Meadery The doors of the barn where the mead was produced were open; Aimee and Chloe were both there, Chloe sweeping the floor and Aimee checking on one of the tanks.

"Hey," I said as I got out of the truck, a pan of enchiladas from my freezer in my hands. "How are you guys holding up?"

"I've been better," Aimee said. "I'm trying to keep busy and not think about it too much, but it's hard. I keep trying to tell Mama Serafine'll be okay, but she may be here before tomorrow. She never wanted us to come to Texas, and now that Serafine's been arrested twice..."

"Did you tell her about the genetic test results?"

"I didn't really have a chance to tell her," Aimee said. "There was a lot of upset."

"I'll bet," I said. "I brought you some enchiladas."

"Thanks," she said. "I'm not super hungry, but maybe Chloe is?"

"I am," she confirmed.

"If you'll finish cleaning up in here, I'll get the table set," Aimee told Chloe.

"No problem," Chloe replied, and Aimee turned to me. "I've got the beeswax and honey for you in a box in the corner there." She gestured to a crate near the door.

"Thanks," I said.

"How are the hives doing? Serafine said you were having trouble."

"I haven't looked at them since all this began," I said truthfully. "I need to get on that."

"It'll keep," she said. "We've all got other fish to fry right now. Speaking of frying fish, will you stay for dinner?"

"I'm afraid I have to get back to the farm, but I can hang out for a few minutes. Why don't I keep you company while you set the table?"

"That would be great," Aimee said, and together we walked into the house. As Aimee busied herself retrieving plates from the cabinets, I set the enchilada pan on the stove.

"I think I found the poison," I informed her as she opened the silverware drawer.

"What?" She whirled around to look at me.

"There was gopher bait in the garden shed."

"Gopher bait? But there aren't gophers at the farm?"

"I know. I think someone put it there to make it look like one of us slipped it into Priscilla's tea."

"What I don't understand," Aimee said, "is how the poison made it into her drink in the first place. I mean, if she grabbed it out of the tub, when would someone have had a chance to poison it?"

"Maybe someone added it or switched out the bottle when she put it down?"

"Maybe," Aimee said. "But who? And if it happened

during the workshop, there's no way Serafine could have done it."

But Nigel could, I thought, remembering how he'd left partway through the workshop. As could Alicia. Or her son or future daughter-in-law, neither of whom I'd seen since the night Priscilla died. "Did you have much to do with Nigel?" I asked as Aimee turned and laid plates out on the table.

"Well," she said, "we did get a few phone calls."

"Phone calls?" I asked.

"Yeah," Aimee said. "Apparently Nigel's wife saw a few texts Nigel sent Serafine a couple of days ago, right after she went after my sister about her workshop." She chuckled darkly. "I'm guessing that was when she came up with the idea of hiring a really nasty attorney out of Houston."

"Serafine has never dated much, has she?"

"I think she wants to," Aimee said, "but pickings are kind of slim around here. You and Quinn grabbed the most eligible bachelors."

"Don't forget Flora," I reminded her with a grin. Flora Kocurek had recently--or not-so-recently--taken up with Gus Holz, who everyone in Buttercup thought would be a bachelor for the rest of his life. The two were deliriously happy, and rumor had it a wedding might soon be in the offing.

"Gus is a nice guy," Aimee said. "But he's not exactly my type. Or Serafine's."

"Chloe was making Bambi eyes at Nigel too," I said.

"I know," Aimee said. "I think she's probably pretty happy he's single now, although I don't think she's delighted that he's smitten with Serafine. I think she's hoping to seduce him away."

"You think she'd really want to date him? She's what... nineteen? He's got to be more than twice her age."

"You never know where love strikes," Aimee said.

"Did Nigel come here often?"

"He stopped by a few times," Aimee said, "but just like she did the other day, Serafine sent him away. Told him it wouldn't look to good if his wife found out about it. And besides, like I said, she told him she doesn't mess around with married men."

"What did he say to that?"

"He asked if things would change if he was single. She told that while he was married, she didn't want anything to do with him. But now that the police have those texts he sent..." she said morosely.

"I know."

"Why did they pick Serafine? That's twice now that she's been arrested. I mean, she wasn't even there when Priscilla died."

"Alicia heard her arguing with Priscilla the other day, and it was Serafine's tea that was poisoned. I think that, combined with the Nigel thing..."

"Well there's motive there, although not strong enough for murder, to my mind, but how would she have had the opportunity if she was teaching the workshop the whole time?"

I shrugged. "I don't know." I paused for a moment, then asked, "You're sure you haven't seen any doll babies around lately?"

"No. And you know that Serafine hasn't touched that stuff--I mean, really touched it--since we left New Orleans. Mama keeps telling her the spirits are going to turn on her. Now that I think of it, maybe she's right."

"I don't think it was the spirits who did this to Serafine," I said.

"What are we going to do if we can't prove she didn't do it? We're having enough trouble with the meadery as it is. We may have to close it up and go home." As she spoke, Chloe walked into the house.

"What's wrong?" the young woman asked, reading Aimee's dejected posture.

"Oh, nothing," Aimee said. "Well, nothing new, anyway."

"You're here pretty much all the time," I said to Chloe.

"Pretty much," she agreed. "We worked out a deal. I stay in the cottage in the back as part of my pay; it's cheaper than getting a place in town, and it's great to be able to walk to work." Chloe was wearing a cowrie shell necklace I thought I'd seen on Serafine before.

"I like your necklace," I told her.

"Oh, thanks." She fingered the shells. "Serafine gave it to me before... well, you know," she trailed off, her eyes darting to Aimee. "Making any progress on getting her cleared?" she asked. "Aimee told me you were working on it and that you'd helped her once before."

"Working on it," I said. "You were there that night. Did you see anything unusual? Anything that might point to who the real killer was?"

"Not that I can think of," Chloe said, still fingering the necklace. "Who are you thinking it might be?"

"Could be Priscilla's doting husband," Aimee said wryly as she folded a napkin and tucked it under a fork.

"Nigel would never do a thing like that," Chloe gasped. "I know he and his wife were a bad match, but they were getting divorced. Why would he want to do something like that when he was going to be free soon anyway?"

"Maybe he was worried she would leave him penniless if they divorced?" I suggested.

"Oh, no," Chloe said. "Nigel doesn't care about money. He's not into material things."

"Well, he sure did marry a material girl," Aimee pointed out.

"Oh, but none of that was going to him," Chloe told us. "She treated him terribly. Always reminded him who had written a check to pay for the house, and that if he divorced her, it would be the quickest route to poverty." Her hand leapt to her mouth. "Oh. I shouldn't have said that."

"I didn't realize you and Nigel were close," I said.

Her eyes darted to the side, and I could see her pale cheeks color slightly. "Oh, we talked some," Chloe admitted. "I wouldn't say we were close, but he's a real gentleman."

"Are you sure you don't want to stay for dinner?" Aimee asked me as she poured iced tea into tall mason jars garnished with sprigs of mint.

"Not tonight, I'm afraid. I still have to milk everybody and start a batch of cheese."

"A farmer's work is never done, is it?" Aimee asked.

"Isn't that the truth," I said. "Hey. Call me if you hear anything else."

"I will," Aimee said. "I got in to see her today for a few minutes. She's holding up okay, but I want to get her out of there."

"Me too," I said. "I'll do everything I can."

"Thank you." Aimee gave me a grateful smile. "And thank you for the enchiladas."

"Of course," I said. I glanced back at them as I headed for the door. Aimee's usually upright shoulders were slumped, and I could see shades of despair on her pretty features. Chloe, on the other hand, seemed more caught up by the excitement of it all than upset. I wondered about her relationship with Nigel. Was she jealous of Serafine? Nigel had made it clear that once his divorce was final, he planned to court Serafine. But wouldn't that be a reason to kill Serafine, not Priscilla? Unless she was worried about Nigel ending up penniless. I waved the thoughts away as I stepped out into the warm Central Texas evening and headed to the barn to retrieve my beeswax and honey.

As I lugged the crate back to the truck, breathing deep the honey-scented air and admiring the spray of yellow wildflowers that accompanied a few late bluebonnets on the rolling hills next to the meadow, I decided I was thinking too hard, trying too much to find a solution to a puzzle when I didn't have all the pieces. The problem was, I didn't know how to lay my hands on the rest of them.

And time was running out for my friend Serafine.

*O*nce I got home, I lugged the honey and beeswax into the kitchen and checked on the house pets. Chuck, as usual, was lingering near the fridge, hoping for a treat. Lucky and Smoky were chasing each other around the kitchen table, attacking each other's tails. Chuck, oblivious, had eyes only for the fridge... and me, the keeper of the fridge door.

I gave everyone a few treats and some love, then headed out to milk the cows and goats--thankfully nobody had escaped, and there were no more doll babies nailed to the fence-- and then checked on the gardens, taking the time to give water to the veggies that remained. I really needed to get on finding replace-ment plants... and figuring out what to do about the hives.

The sun was down and stars came out in the clear sky as I walked down to check on the peach orchard, making mental plans to harvest more fruit tomorrow, then past them, to where my five hives stood. The healthy ones were still buzzing gently, but the two that were having trouble were relatively quiet. I really did need to get those hives squared away.

But I couldn't fix them tonight. I couldn't fix anything tonight.

My overtaxed brain needed a break.

I stood in the cool evening air, enjoying the burble of water in Dewberry Creek and the rustling of the leaves in the breeze. The smell of peaches and sycamore trees was like the best perfume in the world; I stood for a long moment, inhaling the sweet air and listening to the frogs starting their nightly chorus on the banks of the creek, and the whisper of the grass at my feet. Only when Chuck began barking at the back fence did I turn back to the house.

Although I'd told Aimee I was going to make cheese, I decided I needed to put together something homier, with wonderful smells that would lift my spirits. And with a few pints of fresh honey and some peaches in the kitchen, I was sure some peach honey butter--and maybe some muffins to go with it--would do the trick.

I fed Chuck and the kittens, taking a few minutes to enjoy stroking the little cats' soft fur before they began attacking the broom in the corner, then gave Chuck a pat on the head and headed for the kitchen. I began by slicing up peaches, adding them to a pot with water, and turning on the stove, then dug out a recipe for honey muffins. A few minutes later the smell of cooking peaches began to fill my cozy kitchen, reminding me of many summer evenings spent with my grandmother when I was a child. As the peaches cooked, I assembled the muffin ingredients, starting with the dry ingredients in a large bowl, then mixing the egg, butter, and golden honey together in a smaller bowl.

I had just finished combining the two and was turning

off the heat on the peaches when Quinn called.

"How are you holding up?" she asked.

"Oh, as well as can be expected," I said, watching as the kittens knocked the broom over and scared the daylights out of themselves. They jumped about two feet into the air, all their fur fluffed out, then skedaddled into the living room. Chuck, who was at my feet, was unfazed. "I'm doing better than Serafine, I'm sure."

"I know. I can't believe they arrested her. That's crazy!"

"It is. And then there's this other thing..." I told her about what I'd found in the garden shed. "If the poison was in the shed, she would have had access to it; she's over in the garden collecting herbs and flowers all the time."

"Plus that creepy doll outside the house, and the fact that the tea was Serafine's..."

"Yeah," I said as I began filling muffin cups with the sweet, golden batter. Soon, I knew, the kitchen would smell of even more sweet, cozy goodness... and tomorrow's breakfast would be a treat. Maybe I'd bring a few to Serafine tomorrow... and to Opal, who womanned the front desk at the sheriff's office. She might have some ideas I could go on; she'd helped me in the past. "I still think she's innocent."

"Me too," Quinn said. "Who do you think did it?"

"I don't know," I said, finishing filling the last muffin cup, "but apparently Priscilla wasn't well loved within her family."

"No?"

"Her parents essentially wrote her brother--who was originally her cousin--completely out of their will."

"With all that money?"

"They wanted it to go right down the line. She held all the assets in her family... and her marriage. And from what Chloe said, she didn't let Nigel forget it." I tucked the muffins into the oven and set the timer. "I think we've got to keep Nigel in the running."

"If all the family money goes around him, though, why would he kill her?"

"Apparently Priscilla knew that Nigel was sweet on Serafine, and she was considering a big, bad attorney."

"Ah," she said. "Widowerhood might be the easier path."

"Exactly," I said.

"What about Alicia? Peter told me she couldn't stand Priscilla."

"I thought about that, too, but I'm not sure she'd kill her for it. I mean, she could just get another job, couldn't she?" Although with the past-due notices on the bills I'd seen that day, maybe I needed to reconsider.

"At least there's more than one suspect," Quinn said. "Even if I can't imagine Alicia doing something like that. By the way, here's another thing I heard at the shop today," Quinn said. "You know the man who vanished from the Warren house? They're saying now the house is haunted."

"What does that long-ago disappearance have to do with the house supposedly being haunted?"

"The general gist was that it's his ghost. I heard that at night you can sometimes hear... moaning. And that things move around that shouldn't," she added in a low voice.

"Are you thinking of the latch on the door?" I asked, goose bumps rising on my arms.

"Maybe," she said. "I just don't know."

"I don't know either," I said. To me, it sounded made up. I mean, how many people in Buttercup would be talking about a haunted house in a ghost town some miles up the road?

Still, in small towns, you took your excitement where you could get it, and small stories quickly got spun up.

"I'll talk with Serafine about it tomorrow," I said. "See if she's heard anything."

"You're stopping by to talk with her?"

"I am," I said. "I thought I'd swing by and say hi to Nigel, too."

"Let me know how that goes," she said.

"Of course," I said. "I'm going to make some peach honey butter... want me to bring you some?"

"Is that a rhetorical question?"

I laughed. "I'll stop by tomorrow on my way to visit the station," I promised, and hung up the phone, then checked on the peaches.

They'd cooled enough to puree, so I scooped several cups into a blender, turned it on, and then poured the golden liquid into a bowl. When I'd finished pureeing all the peaches, I poured everything back into the pot, along with sugar, two scraped vanilla beans, and some of Serafine's wonderful honey. I couldn't wait to have my own honey to use... and my mouth watered at the thought of fresh honeycomb. If I could get my bees through the winter, the next summer would be full of honey, I thought. I just hoped I'd be able to share the bounty with my beekeeping mentor.

The kittens had finally gathered up the courage to inspect the fallen broom. I smiled at them as I turned the heat back on under the peaches, when the timer rang. I opened the oven, and the sweet, honeyed smell of muffins billowed out into the kitchen. I put the golden-topped muffins on a rack to cool, then popped one out of its tin and onto a plate. With a slather of fresh butter I'd made myself the previous week and a drizzle of Serafine's honey, it was heaven on earth. I was about to eat a second one when Chuck, who had been sitting at my feet watching me with rapt attention, suddenly perked up his ears and growled.

"What is it, boy?" I asked.

His hackles rose as I spoke, and I felt the hairs on my own arms rise. It was dark outside, and with all the curtains wide open, anyone outside would have a full view of me. I reached to the wall switch and cut the light. As darkness enveloped the kitchen, Chuck's growl exploded into barking, and he scrabbled at the back door.

I grabbed the broom from where it had fallen on the floor, then scurried over to the counter and pulled a knife from the block, just in case. Neither would help me against a gun, but they were better than nothing.

As I sat in the dark, squinting out the window looking for signs of movement, I wondered for a moment if I was overreacting. Finding Priscilla's body had put me on edge... and all that talk of haunted houses hadn't helped, either. Chuck was still scratching at the door and barking like a madman. Odds were good one or more of the goats had escaped again, I told myself. And if they had, it would be better to get them back into their enclosure before they managed to let the cows out... and decimate the rest of my peach orchard.

I stood up and tiptoed toward the front door, figuring I'd let Chuck keep barking at the back door while I slipped out onto the front porch. But the moment the hinges squeaked, Chuck rocketed out of the kitchen toward me. I pulled the door shut, but before it latched, Chuck launched himself at it. It swung open enough for him to wriggle through, and then I was chasing him in the darkness, around the house, heart in my mouth.

I rounded the back corner of the house in time to see Chuck stop in his tracks, snarling like a Rottweiler at a figure in black. Something gleamed in the faint light of the moon; it looked like a blade.

"I don't know who you are, but you're trespassing," I said. "And I've called 911," I lied.

As I spoke, the figure moved. Chuck launched himself, and a foot lashed out. My poor poodle yelped.

"Chuck!" I called.

Chuck launched himself again, and the figure swore under its breath; whether it was a man or a woman I couldn't tell. He or she stooped, and something flew from their hand; a moment later, pain exploded in my left temple. I yelped and stumbled, falling to my knees as Chuck lunged at my attacker. The shadowy figure sprinted across the yard and leapt over the side fence, my bald poodle in hot pursuit.

And then he or she was gone, leaving Chuck standing at the fence, barking his head off as I sat cradling my throbbing head.

I stood up slowly, my head spinning, and Chuck returned to my side. I fumbled for my phone and turned on the flashlight app, then looked at the ground to see what had hit me.

It was a chunk of granite. A dark smear rimmed a rough corner of it; when I touched my temple, my fingers were wet and slippery with blood.

"Thanks, buddy," I said to Chuck, bending down to pet him with my clean hand; the world spun as my head lowered, and I slowly stood back up. I walked to the back door gingerly, feeling my temple with my hand. Something protruded from the wood frame.

I flashed the light on it, and my mouth turned dry.

Embedded in the painted wood was the missing knife from the museum garden shed. It pierced a note on white paper, scrawled in bright red marker: STOP MEDDLING OR ELSE.

12

I raced back into the house, locking the door behind me, then turned on the light and checked all the doors and windows, with the creepy feeling that I was being watched. I did a quick glance in the bathroom mirror; my temple was cut, and the skin was swelling and turning red. I made an ice pack, checked on the peach puree, and called Tobias.

"What's wrong?" he asked, reading my voice when I said his name.

"Somebody just stuck a knife through a note on my back door," I said, tucking the phone between my shoulder and my chin so I could stir the puree. "And threw a rock at my head."

"Did you call the police?"

"No," I said, head throbbing. "I... I guess I should." I wasn't thinking straight.

"Absolutely you should," he said. "I'll be right there. Call them right now and call me back; I want you on the phone with me till I'm at the farm."

"Okay," I said. I hung up and dialed the police. A

dispatcher I didn't recognize promised to send a deputy my way. Then I called Tobias back. As he talked to me, I adjusted the heat on the peach butter, then retreated to the bathroom. He made it to the farm in record time, long before the police, and inspected my head.

"You'll have a bruise, but you don't look concussed," he said, looking into my eyes. "Any nausea or vomiting?"

"Not yet," I said.

"Let's keep some ice on it and take some Ibuprofen for the swelling; you need to lie down."

"But the peach butter..."

"I can handle it," he said. "The recipe's in the kitchen?"

"It is," I said. "It's been simmering for about twenty minutes. The mason jars are on the second shelf in the pie safe; I need to sterilize them. Do you know how to can?"

"Of course," he said. "Show me the note, and then you and Chuck need to go rest." He ruffled the poodle's head. "You did great, buddy," he said fondly.

"He did," I agreed as I opened the back door and showed Tobias the knife... and the note. Although I was still spooked, the night seemed much less menacing with Tobias at my side.

"This is serious business," he said, looking at me. "Does this have to do with Priscilla's murder?"

"I can't think what else it would be. I'm glad the police are coming; this points to someone other than Serafine being responsible for what happened to Priscilla."

"Were you asking questions?"

"I was," I said.

"Who did you talk to?"

"The museum director, Alicia. And Aimee. I was at the Warren house today, though, and I thought I saw someone outside."

"What were you doing there?"

"Just... looking around." I told him about the tea label I'd found... and the gopher bait in the garden shed. "I was going to go to talk to Opal down at the sheriff's office tomorrow; I guess I can just pass that info along to whoever comes here tonight."

"I'd still tell Opal," he said. "Is Rooster handling the case?"

"He wasn't at the scene—I hear he's doing more office work lately--but who knows?" I shrugged.

"You spooked someone, that's for sure," he said, looking at the note. "I presume you didn't touch it?"

"No," I said, and walked over and showed him the rock. "Probably no prints on this, but maybe on the knife or the paper."

"Looks like ordinary printer paper... hard to track down. Maybe they can figure out something from the handwriting?"

"Maybe," I said. "It's worth a shot."

We did a quick check of the back yard, Chuck at our heels—I needed to see if there was more damage before I retreated to my bed. Tobias insisted I go lie down as he checked on the livestock; then, as we waited for the deputy, he got to work finishing up the peach honey butter. It smelled divine, and when he brought me a muffin slathered with butter and peach butter, I decided that Prince Charming had nothing on my boyfriend.

The deputy, a young man whose name tag read "Tony Garcia" showed up a full 45 minutes later. He looked to be about twenty, and wasn't impressed by my story... until I showed him the knife in the doorframe.

"Meddling?" he asked. "In what?"

"The murder of Priscilla Jordan-Melville, I'm guessing," I said.

"But we arrested Serafine Alexandre for that."

"Maybe the real murderer's still out there," Tobias said. "And is afraid Lucy's getting too close to the truth."

"Lucy Resnick?" The young deputy narrowed his eyes. "I've heard about you. Some kind of reporter in Houston before you moved here, right?"

"An investigative reporter. And a good one," Tobias said.

"Thanks," I smiled, and turned to the deputy. "I was wondering if you could have that taken as evidence; maybe find some prints on it? I might press charges for trespassing and assault if I can find out who did this."

"What did they throw at you?"

"A chunk of granite from the edge of one of the flower beds," I said, pointing to where I'd found it.

"Can you tell me what happened?"

I went over the events of the evening as Deputy Garcia took notes. "So you recognize the knife?" he asked.

"Yeah," I said. "It was from the garden shed at the Heritage Farms Museum."

"So you think someone stole the knife from the garden shed, came to your house, stuck a note to your back door with it, and threw a piece of garden edging at you?"

"I believe that's what she just told you, officer," Tobias said.

"Right," the deputy said. "This Serafine is a friend of yours, right?"

"She is," I confirmed.

"And I heard a rumor you're trying to get her out of jail?"

"I'm trying to find out who really killed Priscilla Jordan-Melville," I said.

"Uh huh. Well, I guess I can take these for evidence.

We'll see what we can do," he added in a tone that did not inspire confidence.

"You need to take this seriously," Tobias warned him. "Someone threatened this woman and attacked her."

"Well, that is, if she didn't put the knife there herself," he said, voicing what I suspected he'd already decided.

"And hit herself in the temple with a rock?" Tobias said.

"She could have done it herself," the deputy said as he bagged the knife and the note. I was glad Tobias had snapped a picture of the scrawled message while we were waiting, so I could keep an eye out for similar handwriting. I suspected it wasn't going to get a lot of attention once it made it back to the station.

"Look," Tobias said. "This is a serious threat. If anything else happens to her..."

The deputy turned to me with a bland expression. "You got a gun?"

"No," I said.

"Well, if you're really that concerned, I'd think you might want to get one."

"She shouldn't need one," Tobias said.

The deputy let out a weary sigh. "All right, folks, I'll go back and write up the report. Have a good night, and be sure to call if your... uh, intruder shows up again."

Tobias and I watched the young officer saunter to the patrol car; my boyfriend's fists were clenched at his side, and I could hear him breathing hard.

"He totally blew you off," Tobias said through gritted teeth. "I'm going to take this up with Rooster. And the mayor, too, if he doesn't listen to me."

"Rooster doesn't listen to anyone," I said, reaching up to touch his shoulder. "Thanks for standing up for me tonight."

"Of course!" he said. "I just wish I'd been here when it

happened. I want to stay here tonight, in case whoever it is decides to come back."

"I doubt they will," I said. "The message was delivered."

"Still," Tobias said, turning and pulling me into him. "You're too precious to lose. I don't want to take any chances."

"Thank you," I said, burying my head in his chest, then remembering my head was bloody. "Oh... I'm so sorry. I got your shirt dirty."

"Who cares about the shirt?" he asked, pulling me back into him.

I felt my whole body relax in his arms. "I'm so glad you're staying; I wouldn't be able to sleep."

"There's no way I'm leaving you alone after what happened." He bent down and kissed the top of my head. "Let's get you into bed, okay? You need to close your eyes and rest."

"Okay," I said, comforted by his care.

"I don't have to be in until nine tomorrow, so you sleep in; I'll take care of the milking."

"Are you sure?"

"Positive," he said.

A boyfriend who could step in and can my peach honey butter and then offered to get up and take over the morning milking?

Priceless.

Twenty minutes later, I was in under my grandmother's flying geese quilt. Lucky and Smoky were perched on the pillow beside my head and Chuck lay at the foot of the bed keeping guard as I drifted off to sleep, feeling safe and warm and thanking my lucky stars that I'd managed to find my way back to Buttercup.

13

---

*T*he next morning I woke up later than I had in at least a year. Chuck had moved up and was asleep with his back to me, but Tobias was gone; when I checked my phone, I saw that it was 8:40. My head throbbed only a little as I stood up; a mirror examination revealed what my mother always called a "goose egg" on my left temple, along with a scab and the beginnings of some bruising. Tobias had bandaged it for me last night, thankfully; it had stopped bleeding, so I took off the bandage and arranged my hair to cover the worst of it. It was better than it could have been, I told myself as I grabbed my bathrobe and headed to the kitchen.

Tobias had made coffee and put it in a carafe for me, so it was still piping hot. Next to the carafe were several gorgeous jars of peach honey butter and a note. *Hope you slept well; call me when you wake up, please. Love you--Tobias P.S. Chuck already had breakfast; don't let him convince you otherwise.*

I laughed. Chuck was what dog trainers called "food-motivated;" he'd do anything for a snack, and Tobias had been trying to get me to put him on a strict diet since we'd met. I had learned to put the kittens' food on a small table in the pantry so they could get to it and Chuck couldn't; he'd polished off their breakfasts several times before I figured out what was happening.

I checked the kittens' food--they were curled up together asleep in the cat hammock I'd set up in the living room for them-- and then poured myself a cup of coffee and retreated to the front porch. It was a luxury not to have my morning chores to attend to. As I sipped my coffee and watched Chuck nose around the yard, I wondered again about my attacker last night.

Someone didn't want me poking around into what had happened to Priscilla. But who knew I was? The only person I'd really questioned directly was Alicia, the museum direc-tor... and Aimee. Why would one of them want me to stop investigating Priscilla's death?

It wasn't Aimee; she had asked me to help her free her sister. Which left Alicia.

Had she been trying to put me off her trail when she told me about Arthur? She certainly had access to the garden shed, and could easily have taken the knife and planted the gopher poison. And she'd been around--and had contact with--Priscilla the night she died. I thought again of the bills she'd shoved into the folder when I was talking with her. Was something going on at the museum beyond the reloca-tion of the Warren house? Something Priscilla knew about, and was going to bring up to the board?

I needed to talk to Serafine to find out what she knew about Alicia... and Nigel. I also needed to talk to Nigel himself. Although he was on my suspect list, it didn't make sense for him to make a nocturnal visit to my home... unless

Alicia had mentioned to him that I had come by asking questions.

I finished my coffee and went inside, buttered a honey muffin, and layered on some honey peach butter. I took a bite, almost groaning in delight, and poured myself more coffee. I took a few minutes to enjoy the fruits of my labor, then opened the back door to take a closer look at the scene of last night's attack.

We hadn't had rain recently, so there were no footprints in the yard. One of the pickets had sprung loose a bit where the intruder had leapt over the fence; I made a mental note to hammer a new nail in so that Chuck couldn't go gallivanting. I headed back into the house, feeling a chill pass over me when I saw the gash in the doorframe. Who had been so spooked they felt the need to threaten my life?

IT WAS a short drive to downtown Buttercup. As always, I relished the views of rolling farmland and quaint historic houses interspersed with cattle and swathes of wildflowers, as well as the transition to the town's historic square, which featured the white-painted courthouse snugged into the town square's green. It was ringed by quaint buildings housing antique stores, bed and breakfasts, the Enchanted Florist, with pots of bright red and coral geraniums in front of the short picket fence, and the Red & White Grocery, which still featured a few lanky tomato plants for late gardeners. I stopped by and picked up a few to replace the plants the goats had pulled up, then got back into my truck and drove past the Blue Onion cafe, which was buzzing with townspeople hungry for lunch and gossip. A small line had formed outside the restaurant, and I decided to stop by after I had a chat with Serafine.

The sheriff's department was in a small bungalow a couple of blocks off the main square, and there was plenty of parking on the tree-lined street. I pulled under a broad-leafed sycamore tree, and retrieved the small Tupperware container of honey muffins and two jars of honey peach butter from the passenger seat. To my relief, Opal was at the front desk of the sheriff's office. Her eyes lit up when she saw me... and the jars of peach honey butter.

"I was wondering when I'd see you," she said as I proffered a jar of last night's efforts. "How are things down at Dewberry Farm?"

"Well, things have been better. I don't know if Deputy Garcia told you about the surprise visitor I had last night?"

"Surprise visitor?'

"Yeah. Someone whacked me in the head with a rock and left a note on my back door... pinned down with a knife." I touched the swelling on temple.

"Oof," she said. "That looks bad. Did you get it checked out?

"Tobias looked at it for me," I told her. "How's Serafine doing?"

"Well," Opal said, adjusting her glasses, "I brought her a new batch of magazines today, but she doesn't seem to like *Southern Living* as much as I do."

I realized I had left one of Cee Cee James's most recent mysteries in my bag; I hadn't finished it yet, but Serafine needed it more than I did. I fished around and pulled out a slightly dog-eared paperback. "Mind if I drop this off with her, along with some muffins and a jar of peach honey butter?"

"As long as you didn't slip a file into it," she said. "Hang on a second." She reached under the desk and pulled out an enormous metal detector, the kind you usually see being carried by beachcombers.

"You're kidding me, right?"

"Unfortunately not," she said. "Rooster picked this up at a pawn shop a couple months back, and now it's the official security device." She turned it on and ran it over the Tupperware of muffins and the paperback. "All good," she said.

"What's up with Rooster, anyway?" I asked.

"Between you and me," she said, "he's doing some kind of marriage intensive with Lacey; she told him she'd file for divorce if he didn't go along with it. She's insisted he cut his hours or she's leaving, so between doing all the workbooks from the marriage thing and getting home by five for dinner, he's been kind of scarce around here."

"How involved is he with Serafine's case?"

"He looks over the paperwork, and he interrogated her the other day. He's convinced he's got the right person," she said as she put the metal detector away.

"What about the peach butter?" I asked, realizing she hadn't scanned it.

"Kind of hard to get a reading off a jar with a metal lid," she said. She turned it over a couple of times in her hands and examined it. "I think you're good to go."

"You sure you won't get in trouble?" I asked.

"Nah," she said. "Although come to think of it, maybe I should hold onto it, just in case. Rooster and I got into it a couple weeks back over who's supposed to wash the coffee mugs. I won, of course, but I don't want to push my luck." She tucked the peach butter into a drawer. "I'll give it to her when she gets out."

"You think she will?" I asked.

"She's got somebody from New Orleans going to post

bail for her," Opal said. "I'll be glad to see her go: not because I don't like her, but because that's an awful small room to spend your days in. I make it as homey as I can, of course, with curtains and magazines, but reading cobbler recipes only goes so far, particularly when you don't have a kitchen."

"Good point," I said.

"I'll go tell her you're here," she told me, standing up and smoothing down her pink and blue floral dress.

"Before you do, any idea on how things are going?"

She pursed her lips. "Everybody here is pretty fixed on Serafine, I'm afraid. I don't believe she did it, but nobody here listens to me."

"Where's Deputy Shames?" I asked.

"She's takin' a few days off," Opal told me. "Her mom broke her leg, so she's helpin' her out. Well, you met the new addition to the force last night."

"You mean Deputy Garcia? Yes."

"He's a good one, but he's young," she said, "and he thinks Rooster knows what he's talking about. He'll figure it out soon enough, I suppose. The rest of us have."

"I just don't understand how Rooster keeps getting elected."

"Me neither, honey. There's always next time, right?" She sighed. "Last time I wanted to put a yard sign for his opponent on my front lawn, but I figured it might not be too good for office harmony, you know?"

"I know," I said.

"Let me go tell Serafine you're here," she said. Before disappearing into the back, she opened a folder and pushed it to the edge of the desk, then winked at me. As she walked to the back, I glanced down at the folder.

There was a copy of a will in it. The last will and testament, in fact, of Priscilla Jordan-Melville. I looked down at the page Opal had opened to. It was a dispensation of a trust fund. None of it went to Nigel... or to Priscilla's brother Arthur. Ninety percent went to Damian, along with the property and the house, with another ten percent going to the Heritage Farm. I flipped through the pages to look at the date of execution; it had been signed and witnessed only a week before Priscilla died.

Interesting, I thought, as Opal reappeared in the doorway.

"Serafine's ready for you," she said, glancing down at the open folder and nodding as I touched it with one hand. "I'll walk you back."

I followed her down the short hallway to the cell where Serafine was being held. Opal had spruced up the place since last I'd been here, adding a blue rag rug and a new hand-crocheted afghan in blue and green at the end of the quilted single bed. As usual, a stack of *Texas Monthly* and *Southern Living* magazines lay on a small round night table next to a plastic lamp that looked like Opal might have picked it up at IKEA. Serafine looked like she hadn't slept in days, and the bed hadn't been turned down; she might not have.

"Thanks for coming," she said as Opal closed the door behind me.

"I brought you a book; also some muffins and some peach butter," I said, "but Opal's holding onto the peach butter so we don't get in trouble. I hear you're going to be out of this joint soon."

"Apparently so. Aimee got in touch with some of our relatives in New Orleans and they're putting together bail money. If I manage to get out of here permanently, though, they all want me to go back to Louisiana. Who would have thought that a big city like New Orleans would be safer than Buttercup?"

"I want to talk to you about getting out of here. Do you know what they have on you?"

"Unfortunately," she said, "Nigel made the mistake of sending me some texts that the police have their hands on, thanks to some pictures Priscilla took of them with her phone. Plus, Alicia overheard an argument that got pretty heated between Priscilla and me a few days before she died."

"The director, huh?"

"Yeah," she said, rubbing her temples wearily. "Priscilla was pretty focused on keeping the stories at the museum about her family and the people--not the enslaved folks, but the landowners--who lived in their neighborhood. She didn't like the idea of me, who she called an 'outsider,' coming in and teaching about things that weren't 'part of our heritage.' I said what I was teaching really was a part of Buttercup's heritage, and if it really was about the history of the neighborhood, maybe we should reproduce some of the houses her ancestors relegated their unpaid workers--you know, the ones who built the big houses--to. She didn't like that too much."

"Did you tell her you might have been related to some of those... uh... 'unpaid workers'?" I asked, thinking it was an interesting term for enslaved people. Although how do you talk about slavery? It was such a painful thing.

"I didn't bother bringing it up. I haven't met my relatives yet, and now I don't know if I ever will. Besides, the odds that we're connected to the museum's history are not very big."

"What do you know about the tea?" I asked. "Did you give her a bottle? Do you remember her drinking a bottle?"

"I remember she had a bottle of it before the workshop,"

Serafine said. "Chloe and I filled the galvanized tub with tea bottles. She took one then."

"Did she drink any of it then?"

"No. Actually, yes. She did take the lid off and had a swig while she was telling me why I shouldn't be doing my presentation at the farm."

"Did you happen to see anyone drinking a bottle of Arizona Tea?"

"Arizona Tea?" She looked up, a furrow between her sculpted eyebrows. "That's a weird question. No... why?"

"Just curious," I said. "Do you remember seeing her when she came into the barn to talk to Nigel, just before your workshop started?"

"I do."

"I saw her, too. I'd just heard her having a tiff with the director, but I don't remember her having a tea bottle. How long before the workshop did you have your argument with her?"

"About an hour."

"So she was drinking the tea then."

"Yeah. I remember, because she kept playing with the label and folding back a corner of it, and it was making me crazy."

"So she had the tea bottle before the workshop, and then she had the tea bottle when she was found dead, and that was what... two and a half hours later?"

"I guess. I wasn't there," Serafine said.

"I'm curious about the museum director. What do you think of her?"

"She is good people, from what I can tell. She was definitely on board with putting forth the full history of Buttercup and representing everybody who was here, and I respect her for that. I know she risked her job to do it because she thought it was right. I have nothing bad to say about her."

"How were the finances at the museum? Any idea?"

Serafine shrugged. "I really don't know. I know I got an honorarium for the workshop, and my materials covered, and between that and the money they were spending on moving the Warren house, I figured they were doing pretty well. Why do you ask?"

"Just curious," I said. "And this is kind of awkward, but... tell me about Nigel."

"Oh, Nigel," she said, her shoulders slumping. "I met him a couple months ago. At the Blue Onion, actually... I was having lunch. He was at the table next to me, and we struck up a conversation." She smiled. "Chloe was with me; I remember her telling me later how cute she thought he was, which was kind of odd, considering he's old enough to be her father. I gave him a business card because he said he wanted to take a tour of the mead winery. He told me he knew a journalist in Houston who might be interested in doing a write-up on the Honeyed Moon. But then he started texting me and getting a little too intimate about how things were going with his wife."

"Did you text back?"

"I did," she said, "and I'll admit, I was a bit flirtatious. I mean, he is a handsome man, and there just aren't many of them here, but when I figured out who he was and that he was married, I pulled back."

"How did he respond to that?" I asked.

"Not well. He kept at it. He showed up at my door a few times, told me his relationship with his wife was over."

"Had he filed for divorce when you met him?"

"I don't know when he filed, to be honest. I only heard

about it from you. But Chloe told me she thought it was meeting me that inspired him to leave his wife."

"What did you think of Priscilla?"

"One word leaps to mind," she said. "Entitled. I mean, I appreciate that she donated the acreage to the museum. But I realized after a short time that it was less about keeping the history of Buttercup alive and more about paying homage to her wealthy ancestors... and getting a tax write-off, too."

"Seems to be a lot of that in town," I said, thinking of how Nettie Kocurek had tried to get a sausage-nosed statue of her ancestor plunked down in the middle of the town square a few years back.

"Yeah," she said. "So, we crossed swords a bit, but I didn't have that much of a dog in that fight; her main argument was with the director."

"Did anyone else on the board get involved?"

"I think Alicia told me Flora Kocurek was backing her plans, and donated a bit of extra money to pay for the Warren house being moved, but I don't know about the other board members."

Good for Flora, I thought. I really did need to catch up with her and see how things were going with Gus. "Well, somebody thinks I shouldn't be poking around."

"Why?" she asked.

I told her about the incident at my house the night before.

"Oh, Lucy. Be careful," she said, reaching out to squeeze my hand. "I appreciate you trying to help me out, but I don't want you to get hurt in the process. There's a dangerous person out there."

"Don't worry," I said. "I can't afford to eat out much, and I

14

---

*O*riginally, I was planning on going back to the farm, but when I saw a red Mercedes convertible in front of the Hitching Post. I remembered Alicia mentioning Damian getting a Mercedes for his 21st birthday, so I decided to take a detour, just in case Priscilla's son and his girlfriend were there.

Sure enough, when I stepped into the dark little space, which smelled of beer and leather and french fries, the well-coiffed young couple were ensconced in a booth near the back, leaning across the table and deep in what appeared to be in an intense discussion.

Damian's dark hair was tousled in a studied bedhead, while his partner's, equally dark, was expertly styled to frame her face. He wore jeans with a few fashionably placed holes and a dark button-down with pearl buttons; she was in a sundress that hugged her slim form. As he spoke, she played with the straw in her drink, which looked like it was primarily seltzer. He had a mug of dark beer, a third of which was gone.

"Hey, Felix," I said, greeting the bartender.

"Don't see you in here too often," he said. "What brings you here?"

"Just felt like a little pick-me-up," I said.

"How about a Hibiscus Paloma?" Felix enjoyed mixing up cocktails, and was always trying something new, but I didn't feel like getting flattened by a mixed drink right now.

"Sounds strong."

"I'll put it on the rocks," he said. "You'll love it; it's perfect for this time of year. Very refreshing."

"Sure," I said, "if you could get me a Topo Chico with it." I was thirsty; besides, I figured the seltzer would help water the alcohol down. "I'll be over in one of those booths."

"I'll have it right out," he said, smiling and getting to work on my drink as I walked over and slid into the booth behind Damian, pulling out my phone and pretending to study it as I strained to hear the couple over George Strait's "All my Exes Live in Texas."

Behind me, a female voice said, "So when will you have it?"

"I don't know," a voice I presumed was Damian's answered. "I think it's got to go through probate; my mom's attorney told me it will be a while."

"What will we do for money?"

"I asked him to advance me some. He says he'll see what he can do, but he thinks her cousin's going to contest the will."

"What? That weird guy who's always lurking around your mom's house?"

"He lives above the garage," Damian pointed out. "It's not lurking if you live there."

"I don't like the way he stares at me," she said. "He's creepy."

"Come on, Alexis. You're smoking hot," Damian said. "All the guys stare at you."

"Yeah, maybe," she conceded. "Is he still going to live there after we move in?"

"I don't know. My mom always considered him a family responsibility."

"Why should you look after him? You're not even related."

"He's my uncle."

"Yes, but not your real uncle," she said. "Wasn't he adopted?"

"He's still my uncle," he said. "Anyway, this isn't about him; it's about us. Should we sell the place and go back to Houston?"

"I don't know," she demurred. "Maybe we could keep it as a weekend place. It looks great on Instagram to have a weekend place... but we should definitely get a place in Houston. Or Austin, maybe."

There was silence for a moment. Then, from Damian, "I can't believe she's gone."

"And good riddance, if you ask me."

"Alexis." He sounded stunned. "You're talking about my mom."

"I know, but she wasn't good for you. She wanted you to still be her little boy, not to grow up, not to be your own man. That Seraphim woman did you a favor."

"That's kind of mercenary."

"But it's true, honey bunny! You didn't have any interest in law school, and she made you spend the last year taking that LSAT exam and doing all those applications for something you didn't even want. And all that time she's sitting on millions of dollars."

"Not anymore," he said.

"Not anymore," she agreed. "You're free! Now you can pursue photography to your heart's content. You can go wherever you want and never crack one of those awful LSAT books again."

"Maybe. I haven't seen the will yet... there's a good chance a lot of it goes to Dad."

"Well, some of it will come to you," she said. "And the rest will come later."

"Maybe," he repeated, sounding very downbeat compared to his bubbly girlfriend. "Do you really think Serafine killed her?" he asked.

I didn't hear the answer, unfortunately, because at that moment, Felix came by with my drink, which was an attractive blush color, in a tall glass with a hibiscus blossom on top of it.

"I went a little light on the booze for you," he said, "and here's your Topo Chico. Let me know what you think!"

"I will," I promised, taking a big sip of the fizzy water.

"Can I get you anything to eat? Maybe some chili cheese fries, or a plate of our barbecue sliders?"

"Just the drinks, thanks," I said.

"All righty, but let me know if you change your mind!" he said. By the time he made his way back behind the bar, the subject behind me had changed.

"You have to get him to move out," the girl was saying. "I don't want to be there with him creeping around. I think he's up to something."

"Like what?"

"He keeps digging little holes around the place," she said. "Like he's burying things."

"He does help out around the yard," Damian said.

"I know. But I was going down to the creek the other day

to get a shot by the water, and you know how there's that little shed down there?"

"The one with the boarded-up windows?"

"That one," she said. "Well, he was coming out of it when I got there, and he didn't look very happy to see me."

"It's probably just a gardening shed."

"Well if it is, he's awfully worried about losing his tools. He's got about three padlocks on the place; I don't know what he's doing in there, but I'd want to find out if I were you."

"I'll add it to the list," he said. "First I've got to get through the memorial service."

"And we have to plan our wedding, too. And with your mom out of the picture, you won't have to worry about her taking it over."

"I never got a chance to tell her we were engaged," he said dolefully.

"Oh, honey. It's all for the best. She'll be there in spirit, I'm sure," she added in a chipper voice.

"I hope so," he said.

"Come on," Alexis said. "I got a cute new skirt today; I need someone to take a photo of me in it. I was thinking maybe barefoot in the creek?"

"Sure," he said. A moment later, they were headed toward the door, Alexis's arm looped territorially through Damian's. She turned at the last moment and spotted me, and her eyes narrowed; I could almost see her calculating what they had just said, and wondering if I'd heard anything I shouldn't have. Damian didn't turn around, and his whole posture was... well, deflated.

As they disappeared through the door, I took a sip of my drink—it was tasty, but still too strong for me—and thought about what I'd just heard. A few minutes later, I anted up at the bar.

"Didn't like the drink?" Felix asked, crestfallen.

"It was tasty," I said, "but still a tad too strong. I enjoyed it, though!"

"I'll find the perfect drink for you yet, young lady. Come back next time and we'll try you on a blackberry mojito. And tell your boyfriend Tobias I have a new Black Walnut Old Fashioned I think he'll love!"

"We'll be back soon, I promise," I said, thanking him again as I signed my receipt. By the time I stepped out into the warm evening, the red BMW was gone. I didn't think Damian had hurt his mother, but I had new questions about Alexis... particularly now that I knew they were engaged.

And was she making up the part about Damian's "uncle" Arthur digging up the yard and triple-locking a shed by the creek? Or was she just trying to get her fiancé to get rid of an unphotogenic family member?

One thing was for sure: Priscilla hadn't been a fan of Alexis. And it sounded like Alexis hadn't been a fan of Priscilla.

The question was, had she been irked enough by the matriarch's control over her boyfriend that she'd killed him?

I'D PACKED some muffins that morning in case I had time to stop by Nigel's place, and decided now was the time. Quinn had told me the Jordans lived just up the road from the museum, which made sense, since the museum had been carved from their substantial land holdings. I checked to make sure the remaining muffins were still neatly packed into the basket I had put together for the purpose and navigated out of Buttercup's quaint downtown along a country road leading away from our small-town version of civilization.

Priscilla and Nigel's property was just a few miles out of town, past the wrought-iron gate leading to Heritage Farms, behind limestone posts and a metal gate flanked by a high barbed-wire fence. I pulled up to the intercom at the entrance, which seemed to be de rigueur for large landowners in the area, and announced my arrival. No one answered the intercom, but the gate wasn't completely closed. I hopped out of the truck and pushed it open, then drove through and got out to close it behind me. I drove down the winding caliche driveway, passing Dewberry Creek at least twice as it meandered near the drive before I got to the imposing white modern farmhouse I gathered was the new Jordan homestead. I parked in the white carport slung low beside the house, which was cordoned off by a long row of neatly trimmed white roses. Beyond it was a four-car garage built of gray stone and white clapboard, its wooden doors all tight shut. Whoever their architect was had done a good job; the same stone was echoed in the colors of the expensive front porch.

As I walked up to the front porch, I noticed a familiar figure over on the far end of the house; it was Priscilla's cousin/brother Arthur, watering a flowerbed.

I called out a polite hello.

He grunted in return, then returned his attention to the white plumbago he was watering; based on the size of the plants and the fresh mulch, it looked like they'd been planted recently. The whole place looked as if it had been recently finished; the landscaping was gorgeous, but the plants hadn't grown in yet, and the smell of fresh hardwood mulch hung in the air.

A moment later, I knocked at the robin's-egg blue door, the only nod to color on the whole house. It was answered a moment later by Nigel. His white linen shirt was rumpled, as were his khakis; both looked as if they had been chosen to match the interior decorating scheme, which was long planks of dark wood on the floor paired with simple white walls and tasteful, expensive-looking neutral furniture, the robin's-egg blue of the front door echoed in one or two throw pillows on the leather sectional that stretched across the living room to my left.

"I brought you some muffins," I said, offering the basket. I was glad I hadn't put them in Tupperware. "I'm so sorry for the loss of your wife."

He blinked, as if trying to place who his wife was, before thanking me. "Come in, come in," he said, opening the door wider. I stepped inside, catching a whiff of his cologne, which was a mix of sandalwood, fig, and something spicy. "I'm so sorry. I know we've met, but I can't place the name right now."

"Lucy," I said. "Lucy Resnick."

"Ah," he said. "Serafine was helping you with your new hives."

"She was," I confirmed.

"Can I get you some iced tea? Or maybe a La Croix? I have lime, grapefruit, and plain."

"I'll take a grapefruit La Croix, please," I said, and followed him to the kitchen, which was at the other end of the massive open space and featured a large, gray granite island that was almost as big as my truck. "This is a great house," I said.

"Thanks," he responded with a genuine smile. "Priscilla and I had it built after she donated the original house to the museum. Priscilla has... I mean, had allergies, so as beautiful as the old homestead was, she needed something with better air quality for her lungs." He pulled a pink La Croix out of the massive Sub-Zero fridge, popped the top, and turned to me. "Would you like it in a glass?"

"A can is fine," I said. I took the La Croix and handed him the basket in return. He set it on the island without looking at it.

"Please, sit down," he said, gesturing to one of the sleek white barstools that lined the island. "Thank you so much for bringing something. I've been beside myself. I haven't had an appetite since I found out..." He trailed off.

"How long were you two married?" I asked.

"Twenty-three years," he said. "It's hard... I spent every day waking up to someone for years, and then, suddenly, it's as if they were never there."

I wondered if he'd bring up the fact that they were divorcing on his own, so I decided not to mention the subject. "How did you know Serafine?" I asked.

"Oh, we met at the Blue Onion Cafe," he said. "I just happened to be sitting next to her. She started talking with me, and soon we realized we got along very well. There aren't a lot of cosmopolitan people in a small town like Buttercup."

"How did you and Priscilla end up living here? It seems Austin or Houston would be more your speed."

"You're right about that," he said, "but Priscilla was determined not to leave the family homestead. And like a good husband, I acquiesced." A bitter smile flashed across his face.

"How did the two of you meet, if you don't mind my asking?" I said, then wished I hadn't. I still hadn't found out what I wanted to know about his relationship with Serafine. I'd have to find a way to circle back to that subject.

"Oh, we met at a gala, actually," he said. "We ended up sitting at the same table. Priscilla was so beautiful, she couldn't help but make an impression. I invited her to the opera the next week, and it all just kind of went from there. We were married a year later, at Christ Church Cathedral."

"Romantic," I said.

"Yes. I thought we would always live in a penthouse near downtown, but she didn't like the idea of driving back and forth to the ranch so often, so we ended up selling the place and moving here about five years ago."

"What prompted the move?" I asked.

"Her father passed, so she decided it was time to take the reins of the family business."

"What is the family business, if you don't mind my asking?"

"All kinds of things... ranching, oil, property, you name it," he said. "Family's been running things out of Buttercup since they got here from Alabama in the 1800s."

"Was her brother Arthur involved, too?" I asked. Although I knew the answer, I wanted to get his take on family relations. "I saw him outside."

"Oh, no," he said. "Arthur has no head for business. Priscilla was his caretaker, really. Part of the reason she built this house is so that he'd have his own place to live."

"His own place?" I asked, confused.

"He was always asking for rent money, but the money never seemed to make it to his landlord. He'd moved in with us a year earlier. Priscilla built a big garage next door with a large apartment over it so that he had a place to live that wasn't in our house."

Nice digs for a garage apartment, I thought.

"How's he taking the loss of his sister?"

"It's hard to tell," he said. "When I told him, he... well, it didn't go well."

"What do you mean?"

"He said she never should have inherited everything. That his father should have trusted him with at least some of the business." He sighed. "Then he asked if I planned to sell the house."

"I see," I said. Although based on what I'd seen in the file at the sheriff's office, that decision would fall to Damian, not Nigel.

"Not a lot of love lost between Arthur and my wife," Nigel was saying. "Priscilla helped him, but I think the family handicapped him... in psychology, we call it learned helplessness. He was always given enough money to survive, but not encouraged to make it on his own. In fact," he said, "as much as Priscilla complained about him, I think she almost enjoyed having him here on the property. So he could be reminded of how successful she was, and how much he depended on her."

"Lovely family dynamics," I said.

"Her father started it," he said. "She just picked up where he left off. Her father always said Arthur couldn't be trusted with anything." Again, a bitter smile. "I think it was a self-fulfilling prophecy. And as it turns out, nobody could be trusted with the family's business. Nobody except his protégé."

"What do you mean?"

"Oh, nothing," he said, waving the comment off with a manicured hand. "It's just... it's not always easy, being married to an heiress, is all. They come with a lot of family baggage... and you find out too late that your partner isn't really your partner; their loyalty is to their birth family. You're just an expendable accessory."

"That sounds really tough," I said, wondering if Nigel had gotten tired of being "expendable" and decided to "expend" his wife before she could bankrupt him in court.

"I'm sorry," he said. "I... I guess I just have a lot more emotion about this than I thought."

"How did the Jordans make their fortune originally, again? Cotton?" I asked.

"You pegged it. Cotton," he told me. That word said all I needed to know. I knew who had been growing and picking the cotton on the Jordans' 3000 acres, and I knew it wasn't the Jordans. "Of course, once that became less profitable," he said--after emancipation and the boll weevil, I added silently--"they moved on to other ventures. Ranching, oil leases... they've got their fingers in a lot of pies."

"Must have been nice not to have to worry about making a living," I commented.

"Oh, I wouldn't say that," he answered, his mouth twisting down in something like a grimace. "I knew better than to give up my business. I might have married Priscilla, but I was never part of the family. That was made clear from Day One."

"What kind of business are you in, if you don't mind my asking?"

"I'm a psychotherapist," he said. "I have a practice in Houston, and I have a small apartment there, so I was spending about half my time there and half my time here. I started doing some telemedicine lately, so I can spend more time here, getting everything taken care of."

"That's nice, having something of your own."

"You'd think," he said. "But she considered my practice community property. What was hers was hers, but evidently what was mine was ours," he said bitterly, then caught himself. "Sorry. We had a bit of a hiccup about that recently... I guess I'm still sore."

"Community property." I took a sip of my La Croix. "I heard a rumor you and Priscilla might be parting ways."

He cut his eyes away from me. "We talked about it, but we were patching things up," he said, then looked at me with a faux bright smile. I knew for a fact that they hadn't been "patching things up"; in fact, unless something had changed drastically, they were divorcing.

"It must be a lot of work, being the executor of a will with such a big estate."

"Oh, no," he said. "I'm not the executor. Her attorney's the executor." He sighed. "I can't believe Serafine killed Priscilla. I never would have guessed she was capable of it."

"You really think she did it?"

Nigel blinked at me. "It was her tea that was poisoned. And they never got along."

"I hear Priscilla might have been a little jealous of your relationship with Serafine," I said gingerly, taking another sip of my LaCroix.

"What?" he asked, as if that were a startling revelation. "Oh, I know what you're talking about. Priscilla got a hold of my phone and completely misinterpreted some of the things she saw, but there was nothing between Serafine and me."

"Am I wrong that you filed for divorce?"

A shadow crossed his face, and I could feel his body tense from a yard away. "Who told you that?"

"Oh, you know how small towns are." I shrugged.

"It was Aimee, wasn't it?" He sighed. "That woman's had it in for me since the day she met me," he said.

For someone who wasn't too attached to Serafine, he seemed awfully unhappy with her sister. "I noticed Chloe,

Serafine's assistant, seemed rather interested in you at the workshop the other night."

"Oh, Chloe? Just a schoolgirl crush," he said. "I helped her when she sprained her ankle a few months ago, at the museum, and ever since then she's been a little sweet on me."

"Did you go to a lot of the workshops at the farm?" I asked.

"Not all of them," he said. "I was particularly interested in some of the arts and crafts workshops. I often encourage my clients to find traditional activities to bring more flow into their lives and help them curb rumination. When I saw Serafine was creating products with traditional herbs, it seemed like a something I should investigate. At any rate," he said, "you're not here to get my life story, are you? I really do have some things to take care of this afternoon before my next appointment. Thank you so much for stopping by. Can I get you another drink to go? I'm going to get a tea." He headed to the kitchen and retrieved an Arizona Tea bottle from the Sub-Zero.

I blinked as he popped the top and took a swig. "How is that tea, by the way?" I asked.

"What, this?" He lifted the bottle. "I love the green tea flavor. I always say I'm going to make my own, but it's so hot in Texas, the ready-made iced tea is just easier. I go through about five bottles a day of this stuff."

"I'll have to try it sometime," I said.

"Oh, you should. Would you like one now?"

"I'd love one," I said. "Can't drink enough in the summer heat."

He retrieved a second bottle from the fridge and handed it to me. "Thanks again for dropping off the treats... and for the sympathy."

"Of course. Let me know if you need anything else," I answered, giving him one of my cards.

As I walked toward the door, his phone rang. He pulled it from his back pocket and silenced the call, but not before I saw a picture of the person calling. He shoved the phone back in his pocket and held the door for me. "Thanks again," he said, closing it behind me as I walked down the porch steps to my truck, the Arizona Tea bottle in one hand and my La Croix in the other.

When I got to the truck, I set down the can, opened my purse, and retrieved the scrap of tea bottle label I'd pulled from the galvanized tub at the farm. It matched the label on the bottle in my hand. I put the bottle in the cupholder, and tucked the label back into my purse.. As I put the truck in reverse, looking up at the extensive second story of the garage as I backed out, I found myself wondering why, if Nigel's relationship with Chloe was so casual, he had her contact on his phone, and why she was calling him in the middle of the day.

I looked around to see if I could find Arthur, but he was nowhere to be seen. The only sign of his presence was the moist spot on the mulch under the plumbago at the corner of the porch.

My visit with Nigel had raised all kinds of questions.

And a lot of them weren't particularly flattering.

QUINN WAS elbow-deep in dough when I swung by the Blue Onion on my way back to the farm, her red hair swept up in a green bandanna. The lunch rush had finally dissipated; when I tapped on the glass door to the kitchen, she motioned me inside with a toss of her curly red head.

"How's it going?" I asked.

"Busy busy," she told me. "The lunch crowd was huge--everyone wants to catch up on gossip, it seems--and everyone seems to want kolaches today, so I'm making another batch."

"I made peach-honey butter last night, by the way; I brought you a jar."

"Thanks!" she said as I put the jar of golden puree on the counter. "I was going to make some of Serafine's foot balm, too, just as a trial run; if you've got a few minutes, I wouldn't object to some help. I hate spending money on pedicures."

"That was on my list of things to try, too," I said. "I'll give it a whirl; do you have everything you need?"

"In the box at the end of the counter," she said.

"Got it." I opened the box and pulled out a jar hand-labeled Calendula Oil, a block of shea butter, a bag of beeswax, a bottle of sweet almond oil, and a small, cobalt-blue bottle labeled lemon oil. "Are you going to scent it with this?" I asked, holding up the little blue bottle.

"I thought we'd try it," she said. "The double-boiler is already on the stove," she told me. She lifted one arm and used her forearm to wipe a bit of flour from her nose. "How are things with you? Any progress on Serafine?"

"Maybe," I said, and filled her in on everything I'd learned. Including the note left on my back door.

"That's scary!" she said.

"Tobias came over and finished canning the peach butter; he's going to stay with me until we get this figured out."

"Who do you think did it?"

"Someone who doesn't like me asking questions."

"So Alicia, maybe. You didn't talk to Nigel until after the note, did you?"

"No."

"Who else did you talk to?"

"I'm not sure it matters. Someone saw me poking around the Warren house," I said. "I saw something moving outside, but I didn't get a glimpse of him or her. It could be anyone."

"Why is Chloe calling Nigel, anyway?" Quinn asked as she added a little more flour to the dough.

"That's what I want to know," I said. "And do you think Nigel knew Priscilla changed her will last week?" I asked, thinking of what I'd seen on Opal's desk. "I wonder if the old will had him in it?"

"I don't know," she said, "but with all those resources going to the museum, that sure gives Alicia a good motive."

"Particularly with the past-due notice I saw," I said. "Extra funding would go a long way toward taking care of those. Assuming she knew the museum would get anything."

"Do you think she did know? And that she took Priscilla out to make sure the money came through?"

"Probate takes a while, from what I hear," I said. "Although it kind of sounded to me like Priscilla might be after her head."

"You think Alicia killed her to keep her job? That sounds kind of like a flimsy motive."

"It does," I agreed. "But maybe she was hoping she'd get the money to cover those past-due bills... or avoid an audit. Maybe she wanted to avoid going to jail for embezzling, if there was anything funny going on with the finances. Nigel's on the list of suspects, too, but if he wasn't in the will, there's not a huge motive there."

"If she was about to hire a nasty attorney, he may have figured he was in better shape killing her than divorcing her. Did she have life insurance?"

"I don't know," I said, "but I can probably find out." I whipped out my phone and sent a quick text.

"Who's that?" Quinn asked.

"An old coworker in Houston," I said. I still had some contacts at the Chronicle from my former life as investigative reporter. "I promised to bring him a pecan pie next time I was in Houston if he could find out for me," I grinned.

"Good to have friends," Quinn said as I set up the double boiler and put the beeswax and shea butter in to melt, along with the almond oil. I stirred everything together as we talked, bending down to take a whiff of the warm honeyed smell of beeswax.

"I talked to Serafine about the doll baby," I said. "She told me it wasn't her."

"Any idea who it might be?"

"No, but she told me to bring it so she could take a look at it."

"Hmm," she said, putting plastic wrap over the big bowl of dough to let it rest. "So what do you think about Chloe and Nigel? I heard a rumor the other day at the Blue Onion that there might have been some sparks there."

"I don't know what to think," I said. "But I found a bit of an Arizona Tea label in the tub at the museum, and found out today that that's Nigel's favorite drink."

"Interesting," she said, washing her hands, "but I'm not sure how that relates to what happened to Priscilla."

"What if he poisoned a bottle of Arizona Tea, carried it along with him, then poured some of it into his wife's tea bottle when she wasn't looking?"

'I don't remember him having a bottle of Arizona tea at the workshop."

"Of course he wouldn't," I said. "He'd get rid of it; he wouldn't want to carry a poisoned bottle with him."

"What do you think he did with it?"

"Put it in the recycling, maybe? It's worth checking out," I said. "Wanna go with me?"

She glanced at her watch. "Lunch service is over, and everything's pretty clean, so why not? Let's finish that foot balm. I'll put this dough in the fridge and get back to it later tonight."

"Everything's melting pretty quickly, so it should only be a few minutes," I said; the beeswax and shea butter were liquefying quickly, and they smelled fabulous. I stirred as Quinn finished cleaning up the bowls and the last of the dishes; as she wiped down the cutting board, I stirred the calendula oil, honey, and lemon oil into the mixture, then grabbed the metal funnel off the shelf above the stove and filled several small mason jars with the liquid, scraping the pot to make sure I got all of it.

"How's it looking?"

"Liquid," I said. "You're not using preservative?"

"No," she said. "You might want to if you're going to market it, but this is just a trial run for at-home use."

Once I put the lids on the jars, I scooped a little residue from the top of the double boiler and sniffed it. "The lemon's lovely," I said, and rubbed it into my elbows, which were always dry and rough.

She walked up next to me and scooped some up, then rubbed it into her hands and gave them a sniff. "Mmm," she said. "This stuff will be perfect in winter."

"Especially on your feet before bed, if you wear socks."

"It's June," she reminded me. "We've got till January before it gets cold, so don't get too excited. Ready to go to the museum?"

"Sure," I said. "Although I'm not sure how we're going to explain digging through the recycling."

"You could say you think you lost something?"

"Like a poisoned tea bottle?"

"You might want to get more creative than that. When does the recycling come, anyway?"

"Tomorrow," I said. "We'd better get going."

"Sifting through garbage at happy hour? You sure know how to have fun."

"If it means getting Serafine out of jail, I'd sift through worse than that," I said.

"Word, sister," my friend said with a grim smile on her pretty face.

HERITAGE FARMS WAS BUSIER than I'd anticipated when we pulled into the parking lot a little bit later, and I was guessing all the recent news had resulted in more than a few "looky-lous," as my mother used to call them.

"So what's our plan?" Quinn asked as I parked under the shade of an oak tree a good distance from the entrance.

"I think we stop by, say hi, tell Alicia we're going to check the gardens, and then stop off and sort through the recycling," I said.

"Without saying what we're doing?"

"Better to ask forgiveness than permission," I said.

"You're doing the talking if someone comes in and finds us knee-deep in trash," she advised me.

"Got it," I said as we got out of my truck and headed for the entrance.

Quinn and I waved at the museum director as we walked by the office. Unfortunately, she took that as her cue to hurry out and talk to us.

"What are you two doing here?" she asked.

"I wanted to show Quinn the garden," I said. "Also, I, uh, can't find a receipt I need for business expenses; I thought I might check the recycling bin and see if I accidentally tossed it. I cleaned my purse out the other day," I extemporized.

"While you're at it, see if you can find the Jordan brooch," she said.

"What do you mean?"

"Remember how I said some things have gone missing? Well, Priscilla's grandmother's prize sapphire brooch—came from Paris—has also disappeared," she said. "I've been turning absolutely everything over looking for it; it must have been worth tens of thousands of dollars." She sighed. "It's almost a good thing Priscilla is gone; she'd be furious at me."

"I wonder who it would belong to now?" I asked.

"Why, the museum, of course," she said. "Priscilla donated it."

"I guess I was thinking about the estate," I said, wondering what she knew about Priscilla's will.

"Oh, didn't you hear?" she said, smiling brightly. "The executor just called today. The museum is getting a huge chunk of the Jordan fortune, along with more land. It looks like we're going to be the best-funded living history museum in all of Central Texas!"

"Wow," I said, as if I hadn't seen the will on Opal's desk. "Congratulations!"

"I just wish it didn't come under such horrible circumstances," she said, her attempt at a solemn face not looking particularly convincing.

"Me too," I said. "And I'm still hoping we can get Serafine off the hook. You don't think she did it, do you?"

"I just don't know," the director said, shrugging.

$\mathcal{F}$ortunately, the phone rang inside the office, drawing Alicia away. I looked at Quinn, and together we walked on.

"Ready?"

"I even brought latex gloves," she said, pulling them out of her back pocket as we headed toward the fenced-off enclosure where trash and recycling were kept.

"Let's hope whoever it was recycled the bottle and didn't throw it in the dumpster." We both looked at the massive black cube with apprehension. It smelled a little ripe, like sour milk and onions, and something else... something deeply unpleasant. Both of us hoped what we were looking for would be in the two smaller yellow and green bins beside it.

"What did they do with their trash back in the day?" Quinn asked as she opened the lid of one recycling bin and peered in.

"Burned or buried it, I guess. Not a lot of dumpsters back in the 1800s, I suppose."

"This one's half-full."

"So's this one," I said, opening the second bin. "How are we going to do this?"

"I guess we just dump it all out on the ground and put it back in piece by piece," she suggested.

"Glad you brought gloves."

We gloved up and each tipped over our bins, distributing papers, bottles (a few of which were broken), and cans all over the stained pavement.

"What are we looking for again?" Quinn asked.

"Well, an Arizona Tea bottle, for starters. Or any tea bottle. Who knows?"

"But wasn't she found with the tea bottle in question?" Quinn asked.

"Yes," I answered, "but my theory is that the poison may have been poured from another bottle into hers."

"Based on what?" she asked, wrinkling her nose at the pile of recycling.

"Wild goose chase? Desperation? I don't know, but I don't know where else to go from here."

She sighed. "All right, then. Let's get started." We started sorting. As she threw the third half-crunched Coke can into the bin, she asked, "How do we know it's a bottle? And what does the poison look like?"

"I looked it up," I said. "It's supposed to leave a white, powdery residue."

"Okay," she said, and continued sorting. I dug through crumpled museum maps, several juice boxes that had been evidently been thrown in the wrong bin—these I moved to the dumpster. I found three tea bottles, but none of them had Arizona Tea on them, and none of them had any residue that looked like strychnine inside— at least not what Google told me strychnine was supposed to look like. I set them aside anyway.

"This is fairly disgusting," Quinn said, lifting a moldy piece of pizza and a paper towel. "Can't these people read? Recycling, not trash?"

"I just hope whoever tossed it threw the poison in the recycling bin, not the trash," I said, repeating the fear both of us had.

As she spoke, there was a *thunk* on the other side of the enclosure. Quinn and I looked at each other; a moment later, a sour-looking figure came around the corner.

"Oh, hi," I said.

"What are you two up to?" Arthur asked, raising a bushy eyebrow. Although there wasn't much resemblance to Priscilla in terms of deportment, they had shared the same arched eyebrows, and they both had wide-set eyes.

"I think I accidentally recycled a few receipts," I said.

"At the museum?"

"I cleaned out my purse the other night," I told him. "I'm so sorry about your sister, by the way... forgive my manners. It must have been quite a shock."

"Real shock is it didn't happen sooner," he said in a gruff voice.

"Do you really think Serafine is responsible?" I asked.

"That's what the police say. Who am I to argue? If it wasn't her, I'd put my money on that husband she had. I heard her say she was goin' to redo the will. Plus, they were headed to divorce court. He'd hate to have to move out of that big pretty house and work more than five hours a week."

"He only works five hours a week?"

"Why work when you're married to a cash cow? I told her when she met him I wasn't a good idea, but nobody listens to me. Our father always thought she was the brains of the operation, but she was a control freak."

"Doesn't sound like you two got along."

"She always made sure I had just enough," he said. "I'll give her that."

"You think you'll continue working here?"

"Up to the director, I suppose, but she never did like me much, so I'll probably be lookin' for another job soon."

He looked down at the ground, scanning it as if he was searching for something. "What are you looking for again?"

"A receipt for tomato transplants," I said. "I bought some for the museum and some for me; I was going to give one to the director and save the other for my business receipts."

"Well, good luck," he said. He lingered for a moment. "Want some help?"

"No," I said. "We wouldn't want you to get your hands dirty with this. We'll get it taken care of."

"Right," he said. "Well, let me know if you change your mind. I'm headed to check on the garden."

"Got it. Thanks," I told him. As he left, Quinn and I waited until the footsteps had faded before we started talking.

"That was a little weird," Quinn said. "Why do you think he offered to help?"

"Just being nice?" I asked. "Then again, that's the first time he's ever offered to help me with anything."

As we continued to sort, a little breeze came, flipping a torn receipt into the air. I grabbed it just as it was about to blow out of the enclosure. It was for Heinrich's feed store.

"What's that?" Quinn asked as I looked at it.

"A receipt from Heinrich's Feed Store," I said. It was dated four days ago, and included five bags of fertilizer, poultry nipples, and gopher bait. "Look," I said, showing it to Quinn.

"I have no idea what that means," she said.

"It's gopher poison," I told her.

"You mean, the stuff in the shed? The stuff someone used to kill Priscilla?"

As I tucked it into my pocket, Quinn plucked a bottle from the bottom of her pile. "Hey, look," she said, peering at the glass. "Does that look powdery to you?"

She handed it to me, and I looked at it in the light. The glass looked cloudy. "It could be," I said. "Let's hold onto that."

"What does strychnine smell like?" she asked.

"It's supposed to be bitter," I told her, taking the lid off and taking a whiff. It had a strong smell, but I had no way of knowing if it was from the tea or something else. "That doesn't look like one of Serafine's bottles."

"No, it doesn't," Quinn said. "The label's been torn off."

"Could it be one of those Arizona Tea bottles?" she suggested.

"I'd have to compare in person, but it's a definite possibility. I think we should hold onto this, for sure." I dug in my purse and found a Ziploc bag that had once held dog treats, and slid both the receipt and the bottle into it. "Let's finish getting cleaned up and head over to the feed store."

"Why?"

"I want to find out who bought this gopher poison," I said. We finished cleaning up, and as we walked out of the enclosure a few minutes later, we saw Arthur leaning on a pitchfork by the pasture, watching us.

"Should we say something to Alicia?" Quinn asked.

"Maybe later," I said. "I want to talk to the employees at the feed store." A few moments later, we hurried out of the museum grounds and got into my truck, the bottle and receipt safely stashed in my purse.

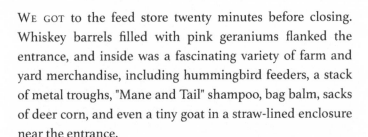

WE GOT to the feed store twenty minutes before closing. Whiskey barrels filled with pink geraniums flanked the entrance, and inside was a fascinating variety of farm and yard merchandise, including hummingbird feeders, a stack of metal troughs, "Mane and Tail" shampoo, bag balm, sacks of deer corn, and even a tiny goat in a straw-lined enclosure near the entrance.

"I love feed stores," Quinn said, pausing to admire several fluffy chicks in a pen on our way to the register.

"Me too, but we're running out of time," I reminded her. Receipt in hand, I walked up to the young woman at the register. I'd talked with Ximena more than once during my many visits; her black hair was close-cropped, and her dark brown eyes flashed with intelligence. "What can I do for you ladies?" she asked as I set the receipt down. "Return?"

"No, actually," I said. "This may seem like an odd question, but could you look this receipt up and tell me who purchased this?"

"Hmmm," she said, eyes narrowing. "Why do you want to know?"

Before I could answer, Quinn blurted, "We think whoever bought this gopher bait may have put it in someone's tea."

"You mean the murder at Heritage Farms?" the young woman asked, perking up with interest.

"You got it," Quinn said.

"Did you recently take a job with the police or something?" she asked.

"No," I told her. "In fact, we think the police arrested the wrong person."

"I'm glad I'm not the only one who thinks that. I know

Serafine," she said. "She's in here all the time; I was shocked when they put her in jail."

"So you'll look it up?"

"I'm not supposed to," she said, "but seeing as it's Serafine on the line, I'll see what I can do." I handed her the receipt and she scanned it. "Good thing I'm here; I think I'm the only one who knows how to do this. We just put this new system in a few months ago, and most folks are still figuring it out."

"Thank you," I said.

"Come by the Blue Onion and I'll make sure you get a free dessert for this," Quinn offered.

"Will work for free pie," Ximena quipped as she typed a few things into her keyboard and stared at the screen.

"Looks like the cardholder is Priscilla Jordan-Melville," she said, then gave us a puzzled look. "Isn't she the one who was poisoned? That makes no sense."

"Unless her husband used her card," I suggested.

"You mean Nigel might be the killer?" Quinn asked, eyes wide.

"Hang on a second here," Ximena said, looking the receipt. "This was purchased on a Wednesday afternoon... let me see who was working." She turned and flipped through a multipage schedule on a clipboard hanging from a thumbtack. "Charles was here," she said, then grabbed a radio from her waistband and held it up to her mouth. "Ximena to Charles, can you come to the cash register, please?"

"Ten-four, Ximena," a low voice answered.

"He's in the warehouse today," she told us as she clipped the radio back to her belt. "He was working the register when the purchase went through."

As she spoke, a lanky, red-haired young man emerged

from a door at the back of the store. "Hey, Ximena. What's up?"

"Kind of a weird question, but do you remember anyone buying gopher bait and poultry nipples last Wednesday afternoon?"

"Hmm," he said. "I wasn't on the register, but I was in the store that day. I remember a guy asking me about poultry waterers."

"What did he look like?" I asked.

"In his 40s, if I remember; no one I recognized. He was wearing a pair of sunglasses, so I didn't really get a good look at him, but he looked more like a businessman than a farmer. I asked him about the gopher bait, I remember. He laughed and said he just about sprained his ankle out on his putting green thanks to the holes they made."

"Putting green?" Quinn asked.

I shrugged.

"Sounds like Nigel. What are you going to do now?" she asked.

"We're going to take this to the police," I said. "Thanks for your help," I told Ximena and Charles.

"Does this mean we'll be in the papers?" Charles asked.

"If all this pans out, I'll tell the *Zephyr* you helped us," I said as Quinn and I hurried out of the store.

"You're really going to take this to Rooster?" Quinn asked as we got into my truck.

"I said the police, not Rooster. I want to talk to Opal."

"That makes more sense," she said. "So Nigel bought the gopher poison, put it in a tea bottle--assuming it was the bottle in your purse," she said, "and then slipped out during the workshop, put it into Priscilla's tea, lured her to the Warren house and locked her in."

"That's my theory," I said.

"Why use her credit card? Why not pay cash?"

"I'm guessing he thought nobody would ever track it back to the feed store," he said. "Or wouldn't link it to him, since it was her card."

"And his motive was to avoid an expensive divorce?"

"Any community property goes to him since they were married when she died. And he doesn't have to split his business."

"And you never heard back about life insurance, did you?"

"No," I said. "But I'll bet he's the beneficiary."

We were quiet for a few moments as we drove back toward the square--and the sheriff's office. I was glad to see Opal's Honda Fit parked outside; maybe somebody with a lick of sense was on the job.

"Let's go," I said, and Quinn followed me into the small office, which smelled strongly of rose potpourri; Opal must have gotten a fresh batch for the warmer on the file cabinet.

"What's up, ladies?" she asked, looking over her glasses as we came in.

"We found out who bought the poison that killed Priscilla," I blurted.

"What?" She blinked and leaned forward, interested. "How?"

"We found a receipt from the feed store in the dumpster," I said.

"What does that have to do with anything?"

"It's a receipt for gopher bait. It contains strychnine, and that's what killed Priscilla, so we went to Heinrich's Feed Store to check it out." I then told her of our discovery of gopher bait in the gardening shed and our discussion with Ximena and Charles at the feed store.

"And we've got a bottle we found in the recycling at the

museum, with some residue in it," Quinn offered. I pulled the bottle in its zip-lock bag out of my purse to show her. "We think it's probably strychnine. Lucy found a bit of Arizona Tea label in the galvanized tub Serafine kept her tea in; and she says all Nigel drinks is Arizona Tea." As she spoke, I could see Opal lean back in her chair.

"It's all very interesting," she said, "but I'm not exactly seein' a smokin' gun here. I mean, yes, somebody, maybe Mr. Melville, bought gopher bait... and poultry nipples, God bless him... but can you prove that's what was in her tea bottle? And just because there's a bit of residue in that thing you took from the recycling..." She wrinkled her nose. "I don't like to think what it might be, to be honest."

I felt myself deflating as she talked.

"Now, I want Serafine off the hook as much as anybody, and I'll take what you've found and give it to Rooster, but I get the feelin' I'm gonna need a bit more than this to convince him."

"Is Serafine still here?" I asked.

"Her parents sprung her two hours ago," Opal said. "Nice folks."

"Well, at least she's out for now," I said. "What else do you think you need to get Rooster to look into Nigel?"

"Well, a confession might help," she said jokingly.

Quinn and I looked at each other.

"Will it count if I record it on my phone?" Quinn asked, a determined look on her freckled face.

"You're not seriously thinkin' of goin' over there and tapin' Mr. Melville while you interrogate him, are you?" Opal asked her, adjusting her glasses as her eyebrows shot toward her hairline.

"You have another plan?" I asked.

Opal sighed. "I don't know. I just work the front desk is all."

"Uh huh," I said, rolling my eyes. "Can you think of any other way to convince Rooster Serafine is innocent?"

"To be honest? I can't." She sighed again, a look of resignation on her round face. "Well, be careful, is all. And for the record, Lucy, I think you may be a few peas short of a casserole."

"Maybe, but at least I'll have Quinn with me. And she's a brown belt..."

"Black belt now," my friend said proudly.

"Black belt," I corrected myself. "So I should be good."

"Personally, I still think a sawed-off shotgun is the way to go, but you ladies are grown-ups. Just don't do anything stupid, ya hear?"

"No promises, but we'll do the best we can."

"Call if you get into trouble. Promise?"

"We will," I told her, and Quinn and I left a moment later, Opal promising to send the bottle to the lab and to keep the receipt as evidence.

"We're really going to see if we can get a confession?" Quinn asked as we got back into my truck.

"Got any other ideas?" I asked as I pulled out of my shady parking space and aimed the nose of the truck toward the Jordan ranch.

"Not really," she sighed. "What's our plan?"

"We confront him," I said. "And we tape the conversation."

"What if he attacks us?"

"Priscilla's murder was with poison," I said.

"Somebody left a knife in your doorframe," she reminded me.

"True," I said. Maybe it wasn't such a good idea. "What else do we do?"

"Did you ever find out about the life insurance beneficiary?" she asked.

I checked my phone; no text or call back from Houston yet. "I'll touch base with my friend when we get there," I said.

"I don't like this plan," Quinn said.

"Me neither," I said. "But I can't come up with anything better, and we have to help Serafine. I'll tell you what... why don't you wait outside while I go in? That way if I get into trouble, you can intervene and call Opal."

"Where do I wait?"

"Outside the house, under one of the windows. I'll give a yell if I'm in trouble."

"All right," she said reluctantly.

We pulled up to the Jordans' gate. Quinn hopped out to open it; I drove through, and she closed it behind us, and we were in.

I parked a little ways away from the house, close to the long, four-car garage. I glanced at the row of windows on the second floor; that was a pretty nice garage apartment all right.

"I'll go first," I told Quinn, "with my voice memo recorder on. You follow once I'm in and crouch under the second window to the right of the door, okay?"

"Why that one?"

"That's near the kitchen; it's where we sat last time I was here."

"Okay," she said. "I'll wait two minutes and then head over. Be careful, okay?"

"Of course," I said, taking a deep breath, stepping out of the truck, and wondering if I should hope Nigel was home.

16

---

*a*s I walked up the steps to the sleek gray and white house, something felt... off. One of the potted asparagus ferns by the steps was a bit off-kilter. When I went to ring the bell, I noticed the door was ajar. The hair rose on the back of my neck. I glanced back to make sure Quinn was watching, then pushed the door open and stepped inside.

"Hello?" I called. Nobody answered.

I walked inside. The house appeared empty, but someone had been here. A bottle of Arizona Tea stood on the counter, condensation beading on the glass.

"Nigel?" I called. Nobody answered. Should I look around more?

I did a quick scan of the open rooms, but nothing looked different than it had when I'd visited the other day. I considered going upstairs, but that felt too intrusive, so I headed back outside and walked over toward where Quinn was now crouched, leaving the door as I'd found it.

"What's going on?" she asked.

"The door was open, but nobody's there," I said.

"Do you think maybe he got out of town?"

"Or just went to the store," I said.

"What kind of car does he drive?"

"I think I saw him in a blue Mini Cooper at the museum the other day," I said.

"Should we check the garage and see if it's here?"

"That feels kind of... trespassy," I said. "And you know how they are about guns around here."

"Maybe we should just... peek in the garage window?" she suggested.

"There aren't any windows," I said. "I know I'm usually the one suggesting we do crazy things, but in this case, I think we should come back later."

"So how do we get a confession?"

"I don't know that we do," I said. "I feel funny about this, though; the front door was open, and one of the plants was knocked half-over."

"That is weird," she said. "Everything here is so... manicured."

"It is," I said.

"Let's at least walk around the place," she suggested. "Maybe he's hiding."

"Maybe he has a gun, too," I said.

"Maybe he's not the only one who has a gun," she said. She opened her purse to show me a small sidearm.

"When did you get that?" I asked.

"I just... well, with Jed and all, I feel more comfortable having something with me. I took lessons on it. I had to get a license."

"Well... I guess so," I said. Something about the house had spooked me. "You know what? Let's just go," I said. As I spoke, Quinn gasped.

"What?" I asked.

"Over there," she said. "Is that... blood?" I looked at where she was pointing. Sure enough, on the corner of the garage was what looked like a bloody smear.

"I'm calling 911," I said. I dialed, and a few minutes later, was connected with a dispatcher I didn't recognize.

"We're at the Jordan Ranch," I said. "Right next to the Heritage Farm Museum."

"What's your emergency?"

"The front door is open, and there's what looks like blood on the wall of one of the buildings. We need the police out here."

"Are you sure the police are what you need?"

"I don't know," I said. "Just... we're going to see if we can find whoever is hurt, but please send a car out. An ambulance, too, please."

"I'll get someone out there," the dispatcher assured me in a tone that didn't sound nearly as urgent as I would have liked.

"Ready?" I asked Quinn.

"I guess," she said, checking to be sure her gun was loaded. Together, we walked over to the blood smear.

"It looks fresh," I said. "And as if whoever it was was headed around the side of the garage," I theorized, looking at the smear; it was in the shape of a handprint. It looked as if someone had grabbed the corner of the house--for support?--and then the hand had trailed off as they moved toward the back of the building.

"There's another one there," Quinn said. Together we crept down the crushed granite path next to the garage; a young wood fern planted along the side of the building brushed my calf, and I jumped.

"Easy, Tex," Quinn advised me from her position two steps behind me, curly red hair bright against her green bandana, patting the gun in her pocket.

I peered around the corner, but there was no sign of whoever had left the blood. There was, however, a short staircase leading up to the second floor, presumably Arthur's apartment. What was going on here? Signs of some sort of upset in the house, then blood on the outside of the garage. Had Nigel been surprised, then rushed out and hid in the garage apartment?

But there was no one else here. Had he hurt himself and gone to Priscilla's brother for help?

"I'm going upstairs to knock," I told Quinn.

"Are you sure?" she asked.

"The police are on their way. If I can help someone in the meantime..."

"Okay," she said. "But I've got your back."

"Thanks," I said, smiling at her. "I'll be back in a jiffy."

I had never been a huge fan of guns--I still didn't own one, despite my country life—but knowing Quinn was behind me, armed, made me much more relaxed about going up and knocking on the door of someone I'd only had about three conversations with. Who might be bleeding. Or dead.

I took a deep breath and marched up the wood staircase. The door had a large glass window, covered by half-open blinds. It was dark inside; I knocked hard on the door. "Are you okay?" I called. "Hello?" I knocked again.

Nothing.

I glanced back to make sure Quinn was still there--she was, staring up at me, gun reassuringly visible in her right hand--and then cupped my hands around my eyes and peered through the glass into the shadowy room.

It was a kitchen; I could make out the refrigerator, a granite-topped island--also with a smear of blood on the corner, as if someone had gripped it--and, on the ground a few feet away, an outstretched hand. Attached to an arm. The rest of the body was hidden behind a sofa.

"There's someone lying on the floor in there," I called down to Quinn, and tried the doorknob. It turned easily, and the door gave when I pushed it, and a moment later I was crouched down next to the bloody body of Nigel Melville.

"OH, NO," I breathed. There was a wound on his head, and he had a black eye, as if he'd been punched.

But he also had a jagged cut on his left wrist, and another, smaller one on his right.

"I found him, Quinn!" I called, touching his neck. I could feel his pulse, but it was feathery, somehow. I cast my eyes around the room, a large open-plan living area with a gigantic television and a sectional, looking for something to use as a tourniquet.

The only thing in the living area was a thick fleece blanket. I turned around... a dishtowel lay crumpled on the counter. I raced over, grabbed it, and tied it tight around the arm with the bigger wound, then started pulling open drawers until I found a second clean dishtowel. As I wrapped it around the other arm, Nigel's eyelids fluttered. I reached for my phone and hit 9, and was about to dial the next two digits to tell the dispatcher we needed that ambulance NOW, or preferably five minutes ago, when Nigel, his face pale, made a croaking sound.

"Stay with me," I said. "I called for an ambulance."

He reached up and grabbed the arm with the phone. "Arthur," he wheezed.

"What?"

"Attacked... Arthur..."

"You feel guilty for attacking Arthur?"

He shook his head. "Priscilla," he said.

"What about Priscilla?"

"Arthur killed..." He gasped for air. "Killed Priscilla. Tried..."

Before he could finish, his eyes grew big. "No..."

"I'm here," I said, and was halfway through saying "It's okay," when something smacked my hand hard, sending my phone skittering across the floor.

And then there was a second smack, one that knocked me onto my side. As my head bounced against the tasteful hardwood floor, the face of Arthur Graham came into focus somewhere above me.

Things were definitely not okay. I was lying half-stunned next to a potentially dying man, staring into the angry eyes of his brother-in-law, who was holding a dirt-caked shovel in his hand. The shovel in his hand must have been the source of the smack, I thought. Then I thought of Quinn. Quinn! She would pop through that door, brandishing her gun, at any second. Or the police would arrive, and hopefully an ambulance with them.

"What happened to Nigel?" I asked, feeling loopy, as if this were somehow a dream bubble that would pop when Quinn burst through the door, or, preferably, the police.

"He was, uh, committing suicide."

"Is that why he has a black eye? And why did you attack me just now?"

"I thought... I thought you were trying to hurt him." His eyes darted around the room.

"Hurt him? I just tourniqueted his arms." I reached for my phone, then realized it was over next to the refrigerator. "Did you call an ambulance when you found him?"

"Did you?" he asked, too fast. Where was Quinn? I felt a cold tendril of fear unfurl in my stomach.

"No," I lied. "I was about to when you interrupted me." I glanced over at the door again.

"Why are you here?" he asked.

"I... I wanted to ask Nigel why he'd bought that gopher poison and poultry nipples. On Priscilla's card." Why was I telling him all this? How hard had Arthur hit me? "Why is Nigel cutting himself in your house? This is your house, right? Nigel told me."

"I don't know," he said flatly.

"Why aren't you calling the ambulance?" I asked.

"Killer," came a dry, whispery voice from behind me. I turned my head to the other side. Nigel was staring at his brother-in-law with something like horror, his right eye red, the skin around it mottled and dark.

And then it all came clear. The gopher bait in the shed. The locked door of the cabin. It had been Arthur all the time.

"I came here thinking Nigel killed Priscilla. But it was you all along, wasn't it?"

"You can't prove anything. Besides, she deserved what she got and more," he said.

"And you set up Nigel to take the fall. What happened?" I asked slowly, sitting up and wondering where Quinn was. "Did he figure out what you'd done and threaten to go to the police? Did he catch you leaving one of those little doll babies around? Why did you do that, anyway?"

"I don't know what you're talking about, but I don't mess with no baby dolls. And he... he tried to do himself in."

"In your house," I said. "After you... fought with him."

"I... was trying to keep him from cutting himself. He came up here and started yelling, holding the knife..."

"Where's the knife?" I asked, looking around. I hadn't seen one. "And why is there blood leading to your place, instead of away?"

"I must have gotten some on me," he said. I looked; his forearms were smeared with red, and blood had gotten under his short fingernails, staining the tips rust-colored.

"Why?" I asked. "Why kill her?"

"I was sick of being a second-class citizen," he snarled. "A serf to her royalty. We were kin, and she and her family treated me like dirt."

I'd heard a similar sentiment from Nigel, minus the kin part. Having a lot of money sure didn't seem to be too hot for relationships, I thought. At least not if you were as territorial about it as the Jordans had been.

"But why now?" I asked.

"She was going to change the will," he said. "Not that she gave me much to start with... a piddly allowance, as long as I kept the job at the museum. Nothing of my own, just an allowance and a place to live. But she went snooping, got into my shed..."

"Your shed?" I asked.

"I was starting my own business. And she was going to torch that."

"What kind of business?"

"Never you mind," he said. "Anyway, once that happened, she called me in and told me she'd decided to give everything--every last cent--to her good-for-nothing son and that stupid museum. And that she was going to evict me. Told me to clear out my shed and get off the property within the month." He shook his head. "I had to get her before she disinherited me."

She already had disinherited him... and he still didn't know it. He'd killed her for nothing.

And now he might be about to kill me and Nigel. "I'm so sorry," I said, trying to look sympathetic.

"It's... it's just not fair," he said, and his face crumpled; for a moment, he looked like he must have looked as the 10-year-old Priscilla's parents had once adopted. "Daddy always said he'd take care of me just like his own. That I didn't need to worry. That if anything happened to me, he'd make sure Priscilla took care of me."

"Only she didn't," I said.

"No," he said. He swiped at his eyes, and I glanced over at my distant phone, and then the door. Where was Quinn? Why hadn't she done something when Arthur came up the stairs and into the apartment?

"Why didn't you just kill her on the spot?" I asked, stalling for time.

"If it looked like I killed her, then I wouldn't get a dime, and I'd spend all my time in jail. I thought they'd think Nigel did her in--that's why I used the tea bottle, and bought the poison with Priscilla's card, but they grabbed that Serafine Alexandre woman instead." He shook his head. "I knew the police were idiots, but man. They really can't tell their head from their... well, you know."

"How did Nigel figure out you'd done it?"

"He started asking questions," he said. "He knew Serafine hadn't done it--he had a horrible crush on her, you know."

"I figured," I said.

"So he was trying to figure out who had. At first he thought it was Alicia--she's been skimming off the top for a while at the museum, and was ready to spit nails when Priscilla told her she was shutting down that new exhibit. But he found out she left the museum and got herself quesadillas at Rosita's while Serafine was giving her workshop."

"So it had to be you," I said.

"He heard us arguin' about the will a few weeks back. Heard her tell me... tell me I wasn't a true Jordan. That if she left me any money, she knew I'd just drug or drink it all away, and that she was doin' me a favor by makin' sure I didn't rely on it." He snorted. "Like that woman did an honest day's work in her life. She always loved holding the strings. What's that sayin', about gold and rules?"

"He who has the gold makes the rules?"

"That's the one. Well, I wasn't going to let her take the family money and give it all to some museum and turn me out of our family home penniless. For all her talk of kin, and honoring kin, she sure didn't give a crap about me."

"She gave you a job," I pointed out. "And a place to live."

"Right. A pittance. You know she's worth like 50 million, right?"

"I didn't know it was that much, no."

"And all she can spare me is a crappy job as a groundskeeper, a few bucks for food, and a garage apartment. While I'm cleanin' public toilets, she's swannin' around town in diamonds and eatin' caviar. If I hadn't taken care of her before she got that new will pushed through, I'd have ended up with nothing."

Only because you let yourself be controlled by the promise of money, I thought to myself. If he'd chosen a different path, instead of waiting for a big chunk later on, he might have lived a free life... and a happy one.

Where were those paramedics, anyway?

And Quinn?

"You're probably wondering what happened to your cute little friend with the bandana, aren't you?" he asked, as if reading my mind.

"Quinn's here?" I asked, blinking as if it were a surprise.

"I got her with my shovel before she could shoot me," he said. "I came up behind her; I'd gone out to the yard to figure out where to put him. Your friend sure is pretty, isn't she?" he said idly.

"Is she okay?"

"She's not dead," he said.

"I lied about calling the authorities," I blurted. "The police are going to be here at any moment; I called when I saw the open door to the house and the blood. What did you do to her?"

"She'll be just fine," he said, in a tone of voice that did not inspire confidence. "For now. As for the police, I'm not sure I believe you, but I'd better get you all squared away in case they do come. Why don't you stand up and come along now?"

"I... I'm not sure I can stand right now," I lied. "You hit me pretty hard." That part, at least, was true.

He raised the shovel again. "I have a feelin' you can figure it out. Now, get up."

I stood up slowly, glancing down at Nigel and praying he was going to pull through. The bleeding had stopped, thanks to the tourniquets, but his breathing was so shallow it was almost imperceptible.

"One more thing," I said. "Did you put that knife in my doorframe?"

"Guilty as charged," he said. "You were pokin' around too much. If you hadn't come askin' Nigel all those stupid questions, he might not be lyin' here right now."

I felt sick to my stomach; I'd been on the wrong path. Arthur was right; my questioning Nigel might have been what caused him to clash with Arthur... and end up here.

"And that voodoo doll on my fence?" I asked.

"Can't help you with that," he said. "Like I said, I don't do the doll thing. Never have. Someone else must not like you very much. Maybe Serafine."

"So if you didn't leave that doll by the Warren house, who did?" I asked.

"No idea," he shrugged. "Don't know, don't care. Now, let's get goin'."

"Where?" I asked.

"Anywhere but here," he said. "Till I can figure out what to do with you."

"And Quinn?"

"Let me worry about your little friend, okay?" he said with a smile I didn't like one bit. "Now on your feet."

As I stood up, I spotted a knife block on the counter by the sink. "Can I rinse off my hands first?"

"No," he said. "Let's go."

With Arthur behind me, shovel in hand, I managed to lever myself upright and walk to the door, mind racing as I tried to figure out what to do. I paused at the doorway and turned to him. "One thing's been bothering me. When did you slip Priscilla the poison?" I asked.

"I wondered if you'd ask that. Well, I'd been holdin' onto a special bottle of Arizona Tea--Nigel's favorite-- just for my sweet sister, all day," he said proudly. "After Serafine started that beeswax class, Priss went to the office to visit the little girls' room and put the bottle on the desk. I doctored it while she was in there, then when she came out, I told her I wanted to show her somethin' down at the Warren house. Once I knew she was taken care of, I put the label in the tub and the bottle and receipt in the trash, figgerin' the sheriff would do a search, find it, and trace the poison to Nigel." He smirked. "Of course, they just arrested that Serafine woman instead, so you found it, not the police."

"So she followed you down to the Warren house while the seminar was going on and you locked her in."

"Bingo," he said. "I even borrowed some of his clothes, dressed up to look like him."

"Then why did you put the poison in the shed?"

"That was a mistake, now that I think of it," he said. "It seemed like the right place to put it, so it would be found. But Nigel wouldn't even know where to find a garden shed, much less use what was in it. I should have left it in his house. But no matter... it's all taken care of, even if it didn't quite go to plan. But enough about me... let's get you down there," he said, jerking his chin toward the door.

"Where are we going?" I asked.

"You'll find out soon enough," he said. "Now, move." He came close enough to me I could smell the onion on his breath. I walked toward the door I had come through such a short time ago. It felt like hours, but I knew it had only been a few minutes. I glanced back at Nigel; he was still breathing, but he desperately needed help. I hoped the police and EMS would be here soon.

I stepped through the door. Sure enough, at the base of the steps, Quinn's body lay sprawled on the ground. I hurried down the steps and squatted next to her. Where was the gun?

Arthur stopped me with a curt "Up!" He was behind me again, practically breathing down my neck. "Stay right there," he said. As I watched, he walked over to the garage and opened the back door, eyes never leaving me. Then he nodded me in. "Go get the wheelbarrow," he said.

The wheelbarrow? I walked into the garage and found a yellow wheelbarrow, scarred with use, up against the back wall. It barely made it through the door; once I maneuvered it outside, he directed me to stop it next to Quinn.

"Grab her legs," he said, and I did. Still holding the shovel in one hand, he grabbed one of her arms, and together we levered her into the wheelbarrow. Her head clonked against the side of the wheelbarrow, and she made a small noise; I hoped we hadn't injured her further. I glanced down at the ground. The gun had fallen out of her pocket and was under a bush.

"Let's go," Arthur said.

"Oh, I... I'm sorry... my head..." I raised a hand to my temple and stepped backward, then pretended to stumble. I fell down heavily next to the bush. Arthur rounded the wheelbarrow, shovel raised above his head, but it was too late.

I had Quinn's gun in my hand, trained at his head. And in the distance, the wail of a siren sounded.

---

17

*T*he dispatcher had delivered, it turned out, and sent both EMS and Deputy Garcia to the Jordan homestead.

"Are you okay, ma'am?" the deputy, who arrived first, asked after my hollering directed him to the corner behind the garage and he had taken Arthur into custody.

"I'm fine, but Nigel Melville's upstairs and he's in trouble. And my friend Quinn is unconscious."

"What happened?"

I gave him a quick rundown of what had happened.

"It's all lies," Arthur complained.

"Then why is there blood on your shovel?" Deputy Garcia asked, earning a few points in my book. A moment later, the ambulance arrived, and as Deputy Garcia cuffed Arthur, one uniformed paramedic raced upstairs to tend to Nigel while another checked on Quinn.

"What's going on?"

I looked up to see Damian and Alexis rounding the corner.

"What the..."

"It's a long story," I said as they watched Deputy Garcia lead Arthur to his car.

"Why is Uncle Arthur being arrested?"

"I'm sorry to break the news, but he killed your mother," I told him, and his face first turned blank and then crumpled. "He attacked your dad, too; he's upstairs being tended to by paramedics."

"What? Oh, no," he said, and hurtled up the steps. "Is he going to be okay?" I heard him ask the paramedic.

"Whoever put those tourniquets on him saved his life," the paramedic's voice came through the door. "He lost some blood, but he's stable. I think he's going to be fine."

A moment later, Quinn raised her head. "What..." She looked around and realized she was in a wheelbarrow. "How did I get here?"

"It's a long story," I told her. "I'm just glad you're okay."

THE MORNING of the Warren house dedication dawned damp and cool, a refreshing change of pace for a June morning in Texas.

I experienced a deep sense of contentment and gratitude as I went about my morning chores, inhaling the smell of the dewy grass as I called the goats and cows to the milking parlor, listening to the chuckle of the chickens as I checked on everyone and gathered the morning's eggs, watered the veggies, and surveyed the remaining peaches in my small orchard. Chuck was at my side most of the time, tail wagging as he sniffed at every tuft of grass. The kittens watched from the windows, alternately batting at the curtains and attempting to pounce through the glass on the birds at my feeders.

Chores done, I processed the fresh milk in the kitchen. I looked down at the beehives by the creek as I worked; Serafine was coming that morning with two new queens for my hives. I glanced at the clock; I only had twenty minutes before I had to be in my full regalia.

I finished with the milk and stowed it in the fridge, tossing a piece of cheese to the ever-hopeful Chuck in the process, and hurried up to my room to change. As I pulled on the voluminous beekeeper's suit, I spotted the fragment of cloth on the corner of the dresser; I never had found out who was responsible for the doll baby on my fence. Or discovered what had happened to all the items missing from the museum. Had Alicia been pawning them to cover her debts? It didn't seem like something she'd do.

I'd barely finished zipping up my suit when Chuck barked, and I looked outside to see Serafine's truck, the Honeyed Moon logo on the side in sparkling gold, bumping up the driveway. I hurried to greet her as she got out of her truck, pulling her into a big hug outside the house. "I'm so glad to see you!"

"Me too," she said, smiling big. "And not a single <u>Texas Monthly</u> in sight this time!"

"Thank goodness," I said.

"And thank goodness Nigel and Quinn are going to be okay, too," she said. "You heard what they found in that shed on the Jordan property, didn't you?"

"No... what?"

"Looks like Arthur was running a little meth lab down by the creek."

"What?"

"I'll give him points for entrepreneurial spirit, at least," she said. "But running a meth lab isn't exactly the kind of business I can get on board with."

"Speaking of entrepreneurial spirit, where's Chloe?"

"Oh, that one." Her smile faded. "I had to let her go."

"What? Why?"

"Remember those doll babies you were telling me and Aimee about?"

"I was just thinking about those," I said. "I never found out who was making them."

"Well, turns out Chloe was the one leaving them all over the place. She found a book about rootwork and decided she was going to do some of her own."

That explained why the scrap of material had come from the Alexandres' house. "Why?"

"Remember that little crush she had on Nigel?"

"I do," I said. "Although it wasn't too little, from what I could see."

"She was trying to turn everyone--including him--against me so she could swoop in and seduce him."

"That explains why she was doing her hair and makeup just like you. She knew Nigel had a thing for you."

"That's pretty much what Aimee said, too. Turns out Chloe was obsessed with Nigel, and was doing anything she could think of to get him to like her. So she left those things all over the place so that people would assume I was the one doing it and then start rumors about me."

"Wouldn't you think being in jail was enough to quash a budding romance?"

"She stopped once I was arrested; the last doll baby she left was at the Warren house. But I found all the stuff in her room yesterday when I was looking for one of the folding chairs I keep in her closet. My fabric, a lump of beeswax, a bunch of pins, and some rootwork book she bought online. When I confronted her about it, it all came out. I asked her to pack up and leave; she was out within the hour. Now I'm fixing the mess she made on social media and trying to undo the damage." She grimaced.

"I'm so sorry," I said. "Any news on Nigel?"

"He'll pull through," she said. "I went to see him in the hospital, and he asked me out." She laughed. "I said we might want to wait until at least a few sprigs of grass grow on his poor wife's grave."

"It is a little early for dating," I said. "But he seems like a nice man. What's he going to do for money now that their son has the house?"

"He doesn't want to live in his son's house, so he's going to rent a place near the square. He's got his practice, and they had some community property investments that are in his name now, so while he won't be rich, he's not going to be homeless."

"Good," I said. "He's going to have to pay for those hospital bills somehow. How did Arthur manage to get to him, anyway?"

"He attacked him in the house when he thought Nigel was onto him. Nigel ran and tried to lock himself into Arthur's place so he could call the police."

"That explains the blood smears around the side of the garage."

"Arthur was too fast for him. He slashed his wrists so it would look like suicide. It was a good thing you got there when you did, or it would have been too late for him." As she spoke, there was a breeze, and a hint of lavender on the air. Serafine froze. "Someone of yours is here."

"My grandma," I told her. "She watches out for me."

"She does," Serafine said slowly. "Now. Enough about

KAREN MACINERNEY

death. Let's get those queens installed so your hives can keep growing."

I ran to get the smoker as she retrieved the queens from her truck, and once she got herself outfitted, we went down and opened the hives. It wasn't long before she had the new queen boxes installed in the hives. I marveled once again at the gorgeous gold of the honeycomb, and couldn't wait until I could harvest some of my own.

"Next season," she promised. "I'll show you how."

"Thank you," I told her. "I wouldn't have tried this without you!"

"Always happy to help," she said. "By the way," she said on the way back to the house. "Aimee told me H-E-B called while I was hangin' with Opal. Looks like they're going to carry my tea."

"That's terrific news!" I said. "We should celebrate!"

"Once the contract's signed," she said, grinning. "Don't want to jinx it."

"Your mom and dad must be so proud of you. Speaking of your parents, when do I get to meet them?"

"We're all going to the opening of the Warren house exhibit. Alicia invited me to come, and told me to invite anyone I liked. My mom and dad are coming... I'd love for you to come, too. I told them about the genetics test, by the way... they're probably going to come with Aimee and me to meet the new family members in LaGrange sometime this week."

"Send pictures," I said.

"I will," she said. "I just can't figure out how I'm related. Maybe we can figure that out, too!" As she spoke, a second breeze wafted by, again scented with lavender.

"I have a feeling you're going to have answers soon," I said with a grin.

"Grandma knows best," Serafine said. "I'd better get back home. We'll check on those queens in a day or two... in the meantime, see you this evening at six! Bring Tobias, too!"

"I will," I promised, and headed back into the house to get rid of my horror-movie beekeeping gear--and call Tobias.

18

The day, which had heated up after the dewy morning, was starting to cool down again by the time Tobias and I arrived at Heritage Farm. I'd told him everything I'd learned on the way to the museum, and he was still absorbing it all.

"So Chloe made voodoo dolls..."

"Doll babies," I corrected him.

"Doll babies," he continued, "and put them up all over the place to start people talking about Serafine so that Nigel wouldn't be interested in her anymore?"

"That's what she told Serafine, anyway," I said. "Apparently she did some social media damage, too... Serafine and Aimee are working to fix it."

"Sad," he said. "People do odd things, don't they?"

"Arthur Graham killed his cousin for money he wasn't inheriting after all."

"I think that was more years of burning resentment."

"Revenge?" I asked.

"It's not as sweet as people think," he said.

"He's going to have plenty of time to think about it in jail," I said.

"I'm just glad he didn't manage to get you and Quinn," he said.

"Me too," I replied with a shiver. "Still, if I hadn't gone over there, Nigel wouldn't have made it."

"That's true," he said. "You do get lucky, my dear."

"Grandma Vogel's watching out for me," I said with a grin.

"Maybe, but don't push it too far," he answered, giving me a quick kiss as I parked the truck.

We walked through the front gate, past the old buildings lining the museum's "main street," and then headed toward the little dogtrot house where I'd found Priscilla.

A small group of people gathered around the front of the little house, nibbling on fried chicken, cornbread, and sweet potato pie—traditional foods, I noted with approval-- drinking bottles of Serafine's tea, and laughing. We walked up and greeted Serafine and Aimee, then met her parents.

"You must be so proud of your girls," I said.

"I am," Serafine and Aimee's mom said. She wore a poppy-red dress and matching lipstick; she had the same curvy figure and big bright eyes as her daughters. She wore her hair up in a graceful chignon, and she had sweet little Jelly Bean, Serafine's rescue Chihuahua, in her arms.

"Jelly Bean!" I said, smiling at the tiny cream-colored dog with big brown eyes cradled in her arms. "She looks better already." She did, too; she appeared deeply content, her eyes half-closed, her little mouth smiling.

"She eats all the time," Serafine said. "And the medicine seems to be working."

"Thank goodness," I said. "Did you find a home for her?"

"She's comin' home with me," Serafine's mother said.

168 KAREN MACINERNEY

"That's wonderful! She looks like she's already adopted you," I said.

"She has," she agreed. "You must be Lucy; I've heard so much about you. I'm Isabelle, and this is my husband, Sam. We're just so thankful to you for finding out who killed that woman. I keep telling Ser it's safer in New Orleans, but she just wants to stay!"

"I hear you have family here," I said.

"Maybe, but nobody can keep these girls in line like their mother," said their Dad, who stood about two feet taller than his wife, and, despite his age, had the build of a runner. Like Isabelle, he'd dressed for the occasion, wearing well-pressed slacks and a sports coat. Serafine was clad in a deep blue silk dress, and Aimee was wearing a purple pantsuit; together with their mom, they looked like a painting.

"That must be one of the families," Aimee said, pointing to a small group walking toward the house; one of the men was pushing an older gentleman in a wheelchair, taking the path slowly. Alicia was with them, her face filled with excitement, and a shadow fell over me; I was worried about financial impropriety, but wasn't sure who to talk to about it.

Alicia, who was dressed in a creamy white suit, spotted us as she came close to the Warren house. "Oh, Lucy!" she said. "I'm so glad you're here; I heard about what happened yesterday. I knew that Arthur was a bad apple; I'm just glad you didn't get hurt."

"Thanks," I said, smiling at her and looking at the group around her. "Who are these folks?"

"Oh! Silly me. Let me introduce you to the family whose ancestors built this house," she said, swelling with pride. "This is Margaret Sims and James Breedlove, and this is their friend Ezra Bilton."

"Wait a moment," Serafine said. "Margaret Sims? I'm Serafine Alexandre."

"You're the one who e-mailed me!" the woman said. "I can't believe you're here... we're supposed to meet later this week in LaGrange! Is this is your family's house, too?"

"What on earth is she talking about?" Isabelle asked.

Serafine turned to her mother. "This is the woman we were supposed to meet for coffee next week! Apparently their family--our family--built this house and lived in it."

"How on earth did that happen?" she asked.

"Let me look at you," said the man in the wheelchair, addressing Isabelle.

"Pardon me?" she said.

"Smile," he told her.

Isabelle reached for Sam's hand and gave the man a suspicious look. "Why?"

"I want to see somethin'," he said.

She smiled--with her mouth at least--and he said, "Well, I'll be."

"What?"

"Unless I'm mistaken, your father was Garland Sims, young lady. He had that same deep dimple in his left cheek."

"You're mistaken, I'm afraid. His name was John Archer."

"Of course it was," he said, grinning. "That was Garland's favorite book character."

"What... how? Did you know him?"

"I did," he said. "He and I were best friends. Only he got into trouble with the law on account of one of the young Kocurek girls takin' a fancy to him."

"I heard about that," Alicia said. "He was acquitted, but rumor had it a vigilante group went after him, and he disappeared."

"That's what happened," he said. "Only everyone was supposed to think he was dead."

"Wait," Serafine said. "You know about it?"

"I'm the one who saved his life," he said.

"Tell us the story," Alicia said, enraptured.

"Well," the man said, leaning back in his wheelchair and folding his bony hands together, "Once the jury acquitted Garland, he was just sure that was the end of it. I told him it wouldn't be, but he wouldn't listen. They came for him, of course. It was at the end of his shift at the Red & White. I saw them do it, and I got in my car and followed 'em all the way to a pasture just outside Buttercup. They pulled into a driveway, so I parked my car and followed 'em in on foot. It was evenin', thank goodness, 'cause there weren't a lot of trees. I could see a fire off down in a little valley, so I ran down the road. By the time I got there, everyone was wearin' those hoods so you couldn't see who they were, and they were all ready to get rollin'. There was a big tree there, and I saw a coil of rope underneath it, so I knew what was comin' next."

"What did you do?" Alicia asked.

"They were just startin' with the proceedin's... they stood him up in front of that tree and then started readin' out charges and askin' how he was gonna plead... and I knew I had to do somethin', and fast. It was late August, so the grass was dry... there were three trucks, all parked right in that long dry grass. So I took my lighter and lit it up."

"The grass?"

"Yes, ma'am. I lit the grass under the trucks. Within about two minutes, that first truck was on fire, and those men weren't too worried about Garland no more. While they were scramblin' to save their trucks, I ran over and grabbed Garland, and we ran hell bent for leather till we got to my truck. I put my foot on the gas pedal and didn't stop till we got to Houston. Then I gave him all the money I had and drove him to the bus station, told him to get on the bus to New Orleans and not come back; I knew they'd get him if they did." He smiled ruefully. "I figgered I'd never see him again, and I was right. But I now I did get to see him, in a way, after all... in his daughter and his granddaughters."

"What a story!" Alicia said.

"So our missing uncle survived after all," Margaret Sims said. "All because of you. Why didn't you tell anyone?"

"I didn't want any word to get around. I knew if they heard a whisper, they'd go after him. And by the time it was safe, I guess I was so used to keeping the secret. Since we had no way to find your granddaddy, I decided not to stir everythin' up, so I kept it all to myself."

"What a story," Alicia breathed, and then looked at Serafine. "I can't believe it was your grandfather's family that built this house."

"I know," Serafine said.

"I knew there was some reason we were drawn to Buttercup," Aimee said, beaming. "An old mystery solved... and lost family found."

"And your family's house restored, and their story told. I'm going to put this in the exhibit, for sure... and I'm think we're going to be doing a lot more than that. I've got big plans, and now that it looks like Flora might to be the chair of the board and we have additional funds from the Jordans, she's going to give me leeway to do what I think is right."

"Speaking of the Jordans, did you ever find out what happened to that sapphire brooch?" I asked, watching Alicia for her response.

"We got a call from a pawn shop after I asked Mandy to write an article about the missing brooch. Turns out Arthur was the culprit; he was cashing in on the family's artifacts. I guess he figured he was owed them."

"I guess so," I said. I still wasn't sure what to do about the past-due bills I'd seen, but I figured I'd tell Flora and she'd look into it. Besides, with new money coming in, they shouldn't be a problem anymore.

"Well," Alicia said. "I think all this calls for a toast, don't you?"

"Absolutely," I said. Alicia grabbed a bottle of Serafine's honey tea and raised it. "To family, lost and found. To the memory of Priscilla Jordan Melville and her family, without whom this museum wouldn't exist. And to the new Warren House Exhibit!"

We all toasted and drank. I leaned into Tobias as we watched Serafine and her family get acquainted with their new cousins; the laughter and excited conversation was a balm to the worry of the last few weeks.

"Well, all's well that ends well," he said.

"I just hope the same can be said for my beehives," I said. I looked at the little Warren house and thought of all the generations who had lived there... and the woman who had recently met her death within its walls. All houses have histories, I suppose. If the house was haunted, it probably wasn't by Garland Sims. If not, who was the ghost? Would Priscilla take up residence now?

"A penny for your thoughts," Tobias said.

"Oh, just thinking about ghosts, and family... and my beehives."

He leaned down and kissed my head. "The beehives mend. Just like that family, over there. They've got some of their missing queens back."

"They do," I said, watching Isabelle, Serafine and Aimee, who talking animatedly with Ezra and their newfound cousins, all of them glowing in the golden light of late after-noon. As I listened to the hum of happy voices, the birds chirping as they flitted among the branches, and the lowing of one of the cows, I reflected once again that I was beyond blessed to live in such a wonderful town... and to have such a fabulous, ever-growing community of friends.

A KILLER ENDING: A SNUG HARBOR MYSTERY

CHAPTER ONE

Two years ago, if you'd told me I'd be spending the day after my 42nd birthday driving north on I-95 with all of my worldly possessions hitched to my Honda CRV in a U-Haul trailer like some sort of oversize snail shell, I'd have told you you were crazy.

But things change.

Boy, do they change.

It wasn't the best time to head out of Boston. It had been after two o'clock on Friday afternoon when I had gotten the last picture of my two darling girls packed up into a box and loaded into the back of the trailer. Since it was the first weekend of summer vacation in Massachusetts, I was now trapped on the highway with several thousand fellow motorists, many of them with kayaks or bicycles strapped to the backs of their SUVs. Like a lot of them, I was headed north to the Maine coast to enjoy a sunny, sparkling summer weekend. Unlike them, however, I didn't plan to come back on Sunday.

Or at all.

Just three months earlier, listening to a deep gut instinct

for the first time in almost two decades, I'd signed a stack of paperwork, plunked down my life savings, and purchased my very own bookstore, Seaside Cottage Books in Snug Harbor, Maine. With the help of an assistant, I'd spent the last several weeks clearing out years of debris from the storage room, dusting the shelves, taking stock of the inventory, and using what little money I had left to add a carefully curated selection of new books. I'd also spent a good bit of time redecorating the place, rolling up my sleeves and repainting the walls a gorgeous blue, making new, nautical-print cushions for the window seats with my mother's old sewing machine, and scouring second-hand stores for the perfect cozy armchairs to tuck away in corners.

The grand re-opening celebration was scheduled for tomorrow night, and I was as nervous as... well, as nervous as a middle-aged, recently divorced woman who's just spent everything she has on a risky venture in a small Maine town can be. I'd used my final pennies (and a small loan) to take out ads in the local paper and spread flyers all over town; I hoped my marketing efforts worked.

From his crate behind me, Winston, my faithful Bichon-mystery-mix rescue, whined. I reached back to put my fingers through the grate and pat his wooly white head; he licked my fingers. "I know, buddy. But once we get there, you'll get to go for walks on the beach and sniff all kinds of things. I promise you'll love it." He let out a whimper, but settled down.

Walks on the beach. Fresh sea air. A business that allowed me to be my own boss. A home to call my own. I repeated these sentences like a mantra, as if they could wipe the memory of the complicated and painful last year-and-a-half from my mind and my soul.

Move forward, Max. Just move forward.

I took a deep breath and let my foot off the brake unconsciously. The car rolled forward and I slammed on the brake again, just in time to avoid rear-ending the Highlander in front of me, which had four bikes strapped to the back. Two adult bikes, and two smaller pink and blue sparkly bikes, one of which had pink ribbons trailing from the handlebar grips. Two daughters. My eye was drawn to the heads in the car: a happy family, going to Maine for the summer. A dull pain sprouted in my chest, but once again, I banished it.

Forward, Max.

By the time I reached the exit for Snug Harbor, the sun was low in the sky and my stomach was growling. I glanced back at Winston, who was still giving me a reproachful look from his dark brown eyes.

"We're almost there," I promised him.

I turned at the exit. Within moments, we'd left the impersonal, clogged highway behind and were heading down a winding rural route, passing handmade signs offering firewood for sale, a sea glass souvenir shop, and a log-cabin-style restaurant advertising early-bird lobster dinners and senior specials. I hooked a left at a T-intersection marked by a large planter filled with dahlias and white salvia. And then, as if I had crossed the threshold into another world, I was in Snug Harbor.

I glanced at Winston; he was perking up as I tooled down Main Street, which was already buzzing with summer visitors, and when I opened the windows and let the cool, fresh sea breeze in, he sat up and started sniffing. Quaint, homegrown shops faced the narrow, car-lined street, which was landscaped with trees and flower-filled planters. Business appeared to be booming; a line snaked out the door of Scoops Ice Cream, Judy's Fudge Emporium was hopping, and lots of relaxed-looking families strolled the streets with ice cream cones and dreamy smiles. Live guitar music drifted out of the Salty Dog Pub as we rolled by, and I caught a whiff of fried clams that made my mouth water. I'd have to splurge on dinner out soon, I told myself. I just hoped a lot of those vacationers were looking for good reads to relax with on their hotel and rental-house porches so I could support my deep-fried seafood habit.

As I crested the gentle hill, passing the town green on my left, the street in front of me seemed to fall away, leaving a perfectly framed view of Snug Harbor.

The water was a beautiful, deep blue, and beyond it nestled the pristine, tree-clad Snug Island; the tide was low, so the sandbar connecting Snug Harbor to the small island across the water was visible. As I rolled down the street, the whale-watching boat came into view; the big white vessel was just pulling out for its sunset tour. Beyond it, I could see the four masts of the *Abigail Todd* as it sailed out of the harbor toward the small, outlying islands.

It took my breath away, just as it had the first time I'd seen it more than thirty years ago, when I'd spent summers here at my parents' camp on a nearby lake.

I drove down to the end of main street and the pier, which was filled with a mix of working boats and pleasure boats (including a few large yachts), then turned left on Cottage Street.

I passed three dockside restaurants featuring lobster boils and fisherman's dinners, catching yet more whiffs of fried clams (this was going to be an occupational hazard), the cobalt harbor peeking out between the buildings and snow-white seagulls calling and whirling overhead in the evening light. There was a little blue-painted shop called Ivy's Seaglass and Crafts, which I knew housed an eclectic assortment of local jewelry and artwork, and then, on its own, a little way down the street, the walkway flanked by pink rosebushes... Seaside Cottage Books.

My new home... in fact, my new life.

I looked at the familiar Cape-style building with fresh eyes, admiring the gray-shingled sides of the little house, the white curtains in the upper windows, the pots of red geraniums looking fresh and sprightly in half-barrels on the newly painted porch. Two rockers with handmade cushions awaited readers. Behind it, I knew, a beach-rose-lined walkway led down to a rocky beach; a beach Winston and I would be able to walk every morning, greeting the sun. And the bookstore itself—it was a dream come true for me. A place where I could connect with other people who loved books, and introduce others to literary treasures that would open up their minds and their worlds.

Pride surged in me at the sight of the book display that graced one of the sparkling front windows—a hand-selected variety of Maine-centric books and beloved reads, including several of Lea Wait's delightful Maine mysteries, two books by Sarah Orne Jewett, a whimsical book by two young women who had hiked the Appalachian Trail barefoot, and —a personal favorite for years—Bill Bryson's *A Walk in the Woods*. They were like old friends welcoming me home, even though I'd just left my home of twenty years for the last time this morning. I smiled, feeling a surge of hope for the first time that day. A sign with the words OPEN SOON was hooked on the door, and I found myself envisioning the community of readers who would gather here.

Goose bumps rose on my arms as I pulled into the gravel drive beside the small building, carefully easing in the trailer behind me so as not to knock over the mailbox. I parked next to the rear of the house, so that it would be a short trip from the trailer to the back door of the shop. And the back door of my home, which was an apartment on the second floor with a cozy bedroom, a small kitchen and living area, a view of the harbor, and even a balcony on which I planned to put a rocking chair and enjoy my morning coffee, as soon as I could afford it.

My store.

My home.

It was the first time in my whole life I'd had something that was completely and totally mine, and I told myself in that moment that I'd do anything to keep anyone else from taking it away from me.

Of course, at the time, I had no idea someone would try quite so soon.

Like tomorrow.

$\sim$

"Hey, Max!"

As I clambered out of the Honda, a bright-faced young woman opened the back door of the shop and stepped out to meet me.

"What are you still doing here?" I asked.

"Just finishing up a few last minute things for the big opening tomorrow," she said. "My mom lent us some platters for cookies, I borrowed two coffee percolators from Sea Beans, and I've got a line on a punch bowl, too."

"You're amazing," I said, smiling. Bethany had been my right-hand woman in getting the bookstore up and running. She'd been crushed when the previous owner, Loretta Satterthwaite, became too ill to carry on with the store, and had banged on the front door two days after I bought the shop. I'd greeted her with cobwebs in my hair—I'd been dusting—and she talked me into an "internship."

"Snug Harbor needs a bookstore," she'd said. "Plus, I plan to be a writer, so I need to keep up with happenings in the industry."

"What about the library?"

"Their budget for new books is meager. I've volunteered there for years," she told me, "but Snug Harbor without a Seaside Books... it's like having a body without a heart." Since I felt much the same way—I'd spent many summer days holed up in the shop as a girl—I felt an immediate kinship. She smiled, and I noticed the freckles dotting her nose and the bright optimism in her fresh-scrubbed, young face. She reminded me of my daughters, Audrey and Caroline, and my heart melted a little bit. "I'll start as an intern; once the store opens, we'll figure something out. I live with my parents and I'm only taking classes part-time. I've got both ample time and a scholarship."

"I can't pay you much," I warned her. "I'm not opening for months and I spent almost everything on the building."

"I'm sure we'll come to a suitable arrangement," she'd announced, peering past me at a jumble of books Loretta had left on a table. "I'll start by rescuing those poor books from their current condition," she'd informed me, and walked right into the store—and into my life.

Thank heavens for angels like Bethany.

Now, as I stood outside Seaside Cottage Books the day before the grand opening, the sight of a cheerful Bethany in jeans and a pink flannel shirt lifted my heart.

"How's it going in there?" I asked.

"Everything's ship-shape," she announced. "I've got the Maine section finished up—two local authors dropped their books by today—and I picked up more coffee and creamer, and some hot chocolate for the little ones."

"Terrific," I said, feeling better already. "Give me the receipts, and I'll reimburse you!" I opened the back door of the SUV and picked up Winston's crate, setting it on the ground. "There is one thing, though," Bethany said.

"Oh?"

"A rather insistent woman has stopped by three times today," she informed me as I liberated Winston from his crate.

"Who?" I asked as my fluffy little dog shook himself all over and trotted over to greet Bethany. He'd been my faithful companion since I'd retrieved him from the pound six years ago, covered in mange and painful-looking sores and looking a little like a scabby goat. With lots of TLC and medication, we'd taken care of the mange and sores, along with the worms and other maladies that had kept him curled up on the couch with me the first few months. Now, he was bouncy, curious, and suffering from a bit of a Napoleon complex, particularly (alas) with dogs that were more than ten times his size. He'd doubled in bulk since I adopted him, and was a terrible food scavenger. To my delight, since the first day at the pound when he climbed shaking into my lap, he'd been my biggest fan, my stout defender, and my reliable snuggle partner. Now, once Bethany scratched his head and got a few licks, he shook himself and waddled over to a tree stump to relieve himself.

"The woman who came by today? I've never met her before, and she wouldn't leave a name. But she was practically apoplectic." I smiled; even though "practically apoplectic" didn't sound promising, I did love Bethany's vocabulary. "She told me she absolutely needed to talk to you."

"Well, I'm here now," I said. "She can come find me."

"Right," Bethany said, but a cloud had passed over her bright face.

"What's wrong?" I asked.

"She said something about you stealing the store."

"Stealing the store?"

She shrugged. "I don't know what she meant. But I got the impression she's planning to instigate trouble."

"Fabulous," I said. "Well, what's a good story without a few plot twists?" This was part of my new goal, which was to look on the bright side and count my blessings. Some days were easier than others. "Speaking of stories, how's your mystery going?" I asked.

"I've gotten to the dead body," she said, "but now I'm kind of stuck. I put the book to the side until after the grand re-opening, though. I've got K. T. Anderson set up for a reading an hour after it starts, and I even talked the local paper into sending a reporter over tomorrow!"

K. T. Anderson was a Maine-based bestselling mystery author who had set an entire series in a town not far from here; getting her to come to the grand opening was a coup. "You are amazing, Bethany," I said, meaning every word.

"Happy to do it. Come see what I've done!"

Leaving my U-Haul trailer behind and feeling rather brighter, I followed my young assistant into Seaside Cottage Books, Winston trotting along at my heels.

The bright blue walls and white bookshelves were fresh and clean, the neatly stacked books like jewels just waiting to be plucked from the shelves. The window seat in the bay window at the front of the store was lined with my hand-made pillows, an inviting nook to tuck into with a book, and the armchairs tucked into the corners here and there gave the whole place the sweet, cozy feel I remembered from when I'd spent summer afternoons in the shop as a girl, when Loretta was still in good health. I walked from room to room, the gleaming wood floors creaking under my feet, and resisted the urge to pinch myself. Where the store, when I first took possession, had been dark and close, the windows covered over with old blankets and the rooms smelling of dust and must, over the past few months, Bethany and I had transformed it into a bright, clean space that smelled of lemon and new books and, above all, possibility.

"I set the table up here in the room with the local books, under the window," Bethany said, leading me to one of the front rooms. "I'm featuring K. T. Anderson's latest, of course. I didn't like it as much as the last one—it's a little heavy on the romance part—but it'll sell well. I ordered lots of stock for her to sign." Sure enough, a table with a light blue tablecloth sat along the wall, two coffee percolators and several platters waiting for the cookies I'd been stocking the freezer with for the last month. Prominently on shelves and tables around the store a stack of postcards was displayed that showed a picture of Seaside Books, including a 10% off coupon and the promo copy we'd come up with together —"Sink Your Teeth into a Good Book—Free Cookie with Every Purchase."

"It looks terrific," I said. "I don't know how I'll ever thank you."

"Become a booming success and feature my first book," Bethany said, "and we'll call it even."

"Of course," I said, grinning at her. I had total faith in Bethany; she was smart, enthusiastic, dedicated, and one of the hardest workers I knew.

I glanced around the store, which was picture-perfect and ready for opening, with pride and anticipation mixed with a little bit of anxiety. After all, everything was riding on this venture. I'd spent the last twenty years taking care of my daughters, running a home, and working part-time at one of Boston's independent bookstores, Bean Books. Now that I was single again, I needed to be able to take care of myself, and after being out of the workforce for two decades, my prospects in corporate America were rather limited. Besides, I couldn't envision spending the next twenty years in some oatmeal-colored cubicle answering phones and doing filing, which was pretty much the only option available for someone with my work experience.

With real estate prices in Boston, there was no way I could pay my rent with the salary that Ellie, the owner of Bean Books and a dear friend, was able to pay me, even though she had offered me an assistant manager position. When Ellie told me Loretta was ill and might be looking for someone to help run Seaside Cottage Books—or even take it over for her—something inside me responded. I'd always fantasized about owning my own bookstore and living in a small community, and I wasn't getting any younger. Did I really want my obituary to say "She always wanted to own a bookstore but never got around to it"? No matter what happened, I was glad I'd gone after what I'd always wanted; and Ellie had been a terrific cheerleader and consultant during my moments of doubt.

Winston seemed to approve of the new digs, too; he'd settled down into the dog bed I'd put beside the old desk I was using as a counter, looking content for the first time that day. Or at least relieved to be out of his crate. I knew the demand for dinner would be coming soon, though.

"Mail is in the top drawer of the desk—there were a few things that looked important, so I put them on top of the stack—and I shelved another order of books that came in today," Bethany informed me. "There was a new one from

Barbara Ross in the order, so I put it in the New Releases display."

"Perfect," I told her.

"I'm going to head home for dinner," she said. "But I'll be back tomorrow. If you need help unloading, I can ask my cousins to come give us a hand tomorrow morning."

"That would be a massive help; there's no way I could get that couch up the stairs on my own, much less the mattress. I can't thank you enough!"

"See you in the morning, then. I can't wait!"

"Text me when you get home, okay?'

"I will," she promised.

I watched through the front window as Bethany climbed onto her bike and turned right on Cottage Street, keeping my eyes on her until she disappeared from sight. Her house was only a few blocks away. I knew Snug Harbor was safe, but I also knew I wouldn't sleep soundly unless I knew Bethany had gotten home okay.

Once a mother, always a mother, I suppose.

"Let's stretch our legs," I suggested, grabbing a leash from the passenger seat of the car and clipping it to Winston's collar. With a glance back at the house—and the U-Haul I still had to unload—we headed down the grassy trail to the water, pausing to inspect a few raspberry bushes with berries hidden under the yellow-green leaves, Winston straining at the leash and sniffing everything in range. Berries I would pick and put into ice cream sundaes, into muffins... I had so many things to look forward to this summer. Beach roses filled the air with their winey perfume, the bright blooms studding the dark green foliage.

Winston romped happily toward the water, smelling all the grass tufts, only slowing down and treading carefully when we got to the rocky beach. The tide was halfway out, and Winston was staying close beside me. Even though the waves in the harbor were minimal, he'd been swamped by a rogue wave once, and had had new respect for the ocean ever since. As we walked, I scanned the dark rocks mixed with flecks of brown seaweed, searching out of habit for sea glass. I found two brown chunks, doubtless the remains of old beer bottles; a couple of green shards; and two bits of delicate pale green that must have started life as Coke bottles; and I was about to turn back when a glint of cobalt caught my eye. I scooped it up and rinsed it off; it was a beautiful, deep blue shard, my favorite color and a lucky find. I tucked it in my pocket and walked up the beach, my stomach rumbling. What I really wanted to do was go to one of those restaurants up the street and indulge in a lobster dinner, but I was on a tunafish budget, so a homemade sandwich would have to do.

I grabbed the overnight case from the back seat of the SUV and climbed the back stairs to the apartment porch, Winston in my wake. Then I unlocked the door and stepped inside, flipping on the light with my elbow, and smiled. It was cozy, sweet, and... in a word, perfect.

In the back of the little house, with a gorgeous view of the harbor, was the living room, whose natural-colored floors and white walls (painted by me) looked fresh and bright, even in the evening. Although the furnishings currently consisted of nothing more than two folding chairs and a dust mop, I could picture how it would be once I brought in my white couch and coffee table, with a big blue rag rug against the golden floor.

The kitchen was small, but cozy, also with wood floors

and white walls, with a card table I'd gotten at the second-hand store in the corner. I'd outfitted the kitchen with odds and ends from my kitchen in Boston, including a toaster oven I'd been meaning to throw away for years, a coffeemaker that had been state-of-the-art in the late 1990s, and stacks of white and blue plates from Goodwill. I plopped down my overnight bag, released Winston from his leash, and grabbed a loaf of bread I'd put in the freezer the last time I was here, tucking two slices into the toaster oven and fishing in the small fridge for cheese. A bottle of cheap but not entirely undrinkable Prosecco sat in the fridge door; I'd bought it in anticipation of this night.

I slapped a slice of cheddar cheese on each piece of bread, then hit "toast" and retrieved a jam jar from the cabinet. While Winston watched, I popped the cork on the Prosecco and filled the jar. Then, jam jar in hand, I walked into the living room and surveyed the view from the kitchen window, which overlooked the harbor.

The sandbar connecting Snug Harbor to Snug Island had been almost swallowed up by the tide, and two late seagulls picked through the broken shells at the water's edge. Two sea kayakers were heading out from the island, paddling toward Snug Harbor, probably anxious to get back before total darkness fell. The sky was rose and peach and deep, deep, blue, and the first two stars twinkled in the cobalt swath of sky.

I looked down to where Winston stood behind me, looking up at me expectantly, head cocked to one side. "To new beginnings," I said, slipping my companion a piece of cheese before raising my jar in a toast, then sipping the fizzy Prosecco. "We made it."

As I spoke, I noticed a furtive figure slipping out of the trees and creeping up the path to the house. Then it paused, and I could see the pale oval of a face looking up at the lit window. As if whoever it was had changed their mind, he or she hustled back into the trees, melting into the shadows. Beside me, standing at the glass door, Winston's hackles rose, and he growled.

Goose bumps rose on my arms for the second time that night—this time, not in a good way. "It's okay," I reassured the little dog, hoping to reassure myself at the same time. "Whoever it is is gone."

As I spoke, the smell of burning toast filled the air. "Drat," I said, and I hurried back to the kitchen, where the edges of the toast had blackened.

I pulled it out of the toaster and onto a plate, burning myself in the process, and cut off the edges with a butter knife, then sat down at the table with my sad-looking toasted cheese sandwich and a jam jar of Prosecco, still wondering who had headed up the path and changed tack at the last minute.

Whoever it was was gone, I told myself as I bit into my sandwich. And I had other things to worry about.

Like unpacking the truck.

And preparing to have all of Snug Harbor descend on my fledgling bookstore in less than 24 hours.

It was almost midnight by the time I curled up with Winston snuggled into the crook of my arm. I hoped it was my last night sleeping on an air mattress, but with my crisp blue and white percale sheets, fluffy blanket, and soft pillows, it wasn't exactly a hardship. Besides, it was lovely being able to see the stars out my window; and to open the window and hear the lap of the water against the shore and the breeze in the maple tree next to the house, instead of Boston traffic in the distance.

I read one of Lee Strauss' charming Ginger Gold books until my eyes started to droop. Then I reached to turn off the lamp I'd set up next to the head of the mattress and burrowed into the covers, lulled to sleep by Winston's steady breathing and the soothing sound of the ocean.

Until a crashing sound from downstairs woke me up.

Download your copy of the first Snug Harbor Mystery, A Killer Ending, now to find out what happens next!

MORE BOOKS BY KAREN MACINERNEY

To download a free book and receive members-only outtakes, giveaways, short stories, recipes, and updates, join Karen's Reader's Circle at www.karenmacinerney.com! You can also join her Facebook community; she often hosts giveaways and loves getting to know her readers there.

And don't forget to follow her on BookBub to get newsflashes on new releases!

The Snug Harbor Mysteries
  A Killer Ending
  Inked Out (Winter 2020/2021)

The Gray Whale Inn Mysteries
  Murder on the Rocks
  Dead and Berried
  Murder Most Maine
  Berried to the Hilt
  Brush With Death
  Death Runs Adrift

Whale of a Crime
Claws for Alarm
Scone Cold Dead
Anchored Inn
Gray Whale Inn Mystery #11 (2021)
Cookbook: The Gray Whale Inn Kitchen
Four Seasons of Mystery (A Gray Whale Inn Collection)
Blueberry Blues (A Gray Whale Inn Short Story)
Pumpkin Pied (A Gray Whale Inn Short Story)
Iced Inn (A Gray Whale Inn Short Story)
Lupine Lies (A Gray Whale Inn Short Story)

The Dewberry Farm Mysteries

Killer Jam
Fatal Frost
Deadly Brew
Mistletoe Murder
Dyeing Season
Wicked Harvest
Sweet Revenge
Slay Bells Ring: A Dewberry Farm Christmas Story (Fall 2020)
Cookbook: Lucy's Farmhouse Kitchen

The Margie Peterson Mysteries

Mother's Day Out
Mother Knows Best
Mother's Little Helper

Wolves and the City

Howling at the Moon
On the Prowl
Leader of the Pack

RECIPES

SWEET TEXAS CORNBREAD

Wonderful with Hoppin' John, particularly on a cold winter day. Or just butter. Lots and lots of butter. And a touch of honey if you're feeling decadent.

Ingredients:

- 1 cup flour
- 1 cup yellow cornmeal
- 1/3-2/3 cup sugar (depending on how sweet you like it)
- 1 teaspoon. salt
- 2 teaspoons baking powder
- 2 eggs
- 1 cup milk
- 1/3 c. plus 2 teaspoons vegetable oil
- 1 teaspoon vanilla

Directions:

Preheat the oven to 400 degrees. In a small bowl, without stirring, soak cornmeal in milk for 15 minutes. Spray a 10-inch round oven-proof skillet or pan (cast iron is ideal).

In a large bowl, combine the flour, sugar, salt and baking powder with a whisk. Stir in eggs, cornmeal and milk mixture, vegetable oil, and vanilla, mixing until just combined. (Batter will be slightly lumpy.) Pour batter into prepared pan and bake for 20-25 minutes, or until a toothpick inserted into center of the cornbread comes out clean.

HOPPIN' JOHN

This old-fashioned recipe is a classic; it's a tasty, easy dish you can toss in the crockpot. I love it with cornbread to sop up the juices, and maybe a salad on the side if I'm feeling industrious. Collard greens are traditional, and you can pass a bottle of tabasco around the table for those who like a little bit of heat.

Ingredients:

- 1 pound black-eyed peas, soaked overnight in cold water and drained
- 1 medium yellow onion, diced
- 1 rib celery, diced
- 1 medium red bell pepper, diced
- 1 smoked ham hock
- 32 ounces chicken broth
- 2 whole bay leaves
- 3-5 cloves garlic, minced
- 1 teaspoon black pepper

- 1 teaspoon smoked paprika

Directions:

1. In a 6-quart or larger crockpot, combine the soaked black-eyed peas, onion, celery, red bell pepper, ham hock, chicken stock, bay leaves, garlic, black pepper, and smoked paprika.
2. Cover and cook on low for 7 to 8 hours or on high for 4 to 5 hours, until the beans are tender.
3. Discard the ham hock and bay leaves.
4. Serve with hot rice or cornbread (see recipe for Sweet Texas Cornbread in Breads and Rolls).

TEXAS PEACH COBBLER

This is wonderful on its own, but even better with a big scoop of vanilla ice cream!

Ingredients:

Filling

- 4 cups peaches (frozen, or ripe, sliced and peeled)
- 1/2 teaspoon vanilla
- 1 tablespoon lemon juice
- 4 tablespoons sugar

Batter

- 1 1/4 cups all-purpose flour
- 6 tablespoons melted butter
- 3/4 cup sugar
- 2 tablespoons baking powder
- 1/2 teaspoon salt
- 1 teaspoon cinnamon

- 1 cup milk
- 1 teaspoon vanilla
- 1 tablespoon turbinado sugar

Directions:

1. Preheat oven to 350 degrees, and peel the peaches if using fresh. (To peel fresh peaches, blanch them in boiling water briefly; this will make peeling a cinch.)
2. Combine the peaches with sugar, lemon juice & vanilla to make the cobbler filling and set aside.
3. Pour butter into an 8-inch square baking dish, making sure it covers the bottom.
4. Combine flour, sugar, baking powder, salt, and cinnamon in a medium bowl. In a small bowl, mix milk and 1/2 tsp. vanilla together. Add milk mixture to flour mixture, stirring just until moist. Spoon batter mixture over butter and spread evenly. Do not stir!
5. Spoon the peach mixture over the batter, gently pressing the peaches into batter.
6. Bake at 350 degrees for 40 minutes, sprinkle with turbinado sugar, then bake for an additional 10 minutes or until the crust is golden.

HONEY MUFFINS

Quick, easy, and oh-so delicious.

Ingredients:

- 2 cups all-purpose flour
- 1/2 cup sugar
- 3 teaspoons baking powder
- 1/2 teaspoon salt
- 1 large egg, room temperature
- 1 cup 2% milk
- 1/4 cup butter, melted
- 1/4 cup honey, preferably from a local producer

Directions

1. Preheat oven to 400° and prepare muffin pan by greasing them or filling with muffin cup liners.

2. In a large bowl, combine flour, sugar, baking powder and salt.
3. In a separate bowl, combine egg, milk, butter and honey.
4. Stir into dry ingredients just until moistened.
5. Fill muffin cups three-fourths full and bake on the middle rack until a toothpick inserted in center comes out clean, 15-18 minutes. Cool 5 minutes before removing from pan to a wire rack.

PEACH HONEY BUTTER

Heaven in a jar. Also good made with apricots!

Ingredients

- 9 cups sliced peaches, pitted but not peeled
- 1/4 cup water
- 2 1/4 cup granulated sugar
- 3/4 cup honey
- 2 vanilla beans, seeds scraped out

Instructions

1. Combine peaches and water in a large pot (I like to use a large stock pot).
2. Bring to a boil and reduce heat, then cover and simmer for 10 - 15 minutes or until peaches are tender. Remove pot from heat and cool slightly.
3. Use a food processor or blender (I use an

immersion blender) to puree peach mixture until smooth. (You may have to do it in batches if you're not using an immersion blender.) You should have about 14 cups of pureed peaches.

4. Return peach puree to pot.
5. Add sugar, honey, vanilla bean seeds, and empty vanilla pod, then bring to boil, stirring until sugar dissolves.
6. Reduce heat and simmer uncovered for about 60 minutes, stirring often, until the mixture is thick and mounds on a spoon.
7. Remove vanilla pods.
8. Ladle hot peach butter into hot, sterilized half-pint jars, leaving a 1/4 inch headspace.
9. Wipe jar rims and adjust lids.
10. Process filled jars in a boiling water canner (I use a stock pot with a metal trivet or dish towel in the bottom) for 5 minutes. Start timing when water returns to boiling.
11. Remove jars from canner and cool on wire racks. Enjoy and give to friends

BEESWAX FOOT BALM

This is perfect for cracked feet and dry elbows. I like to put it on after a bath and wear socks overnight!

Ingredients

- 1/2 cup beeswax pellets or broken-up beeswax
- 1/2 cup cocoa butter discs or shea butter
- 1/4 cup calendula oil
- 1/4 cup sweet almond oil
- 30 drops lavender or other essential oil
- Glass or metal jars with lids

Instructions

1. Bring water in bottom of a double boiler to a boil, then reduce to a simmer.
2. Place all ingredients (except essential oil) in the top pan of the double boiler.

3. Heat ingredients, swirling the pan from time to time, allowing beeswax pellets and cocoa butter discs to melt completely.

4. Remove from heat and add lavender essential oil. Swirl to mix.

5. Pour liquid into containers and allow to cool, then put on lids.

SERAFINE'S SALVE

This is a two-part recipe, if you want to make your own herb-infused oil. You can also purchase your infused oil premade if you want to skip to the second step. And, as always, the recommendations below are not meant to be medical advice!

Infused Herbal Oil

Ingredients

- Almond, olive, or grapeseed oil
- Clean, dry 1-quart jar
- Dried herbs or flowers, in enough quantity to fill jar 2/3 full

Directions

NOTE: Serafine recommends using only dried herbs in your infusions, as the lack of moisture content in the plant material can keep spoilage at bay.

1. Place dried herbs or flowers in a clean, dry quart jar, leaving at least 1 to 3 inches of open space above the plant material.
2. Fill the jar with your oil of choice, making sure to cover herbs by at least 1 inch or more. If the herbs emerge above the surface of the oil at any point while infusing, pour more oil on top to ensure the herbs remain covered.
3. Cap the jar tightly and shake well.
4. Place jar in a sunny, warm windowsill and shake once or more per day. Covering the oil with a paper bag can help prevent UV light-induced degradation.
5. After 2 to 3 weeks, strain the herbs out of the oil using cheesecloth or a mesh strainer, using pressure to squeeze out as much of the oil as possible.
6. Pour oil into clean glass bottles or jars, and label with date and type of herb.
7. Store in a cool, dark place. The oil may keep for up to a year.

Salve

Ingredients

- 1 oz. beeswax bar or pellets
- 4 oz. herbal infused oil(s)
- 10-20 drops essential oil for fragrance (optional)
- Small, clean jars or tins

Directions

1. If using bar beeswax, wrap bar in an old tea towel. On a cutting board or counter, use a mallet to break the bar up into small chunks.
2. Place the beeswax in a double boiler and warm over low heat until the beeswax melts.
3. Once beeswax has melted, add herbal oils and stir over low heat until well-mixed.
4. Remove from heat and swirl in the essential oil (if using).
5. Quickly pour warm mixture into tins or jars and allow to cool completely, then put on lids.

Note: Use less beeswax for a softer salve and more beeswax if you'd like it harder; to test the consistency, put a spoon in the freezer, then pour a little salve onto the cold spoons and put it back into the freezer for 1 to 2 minutes. This will give you a feel for what the final consistency will be like. Once the salve has cooled, if you need to, you can make adjustments by adding more oil to soften it or more beeswax to harden it.

Other Salve Ideas

- Arnica flowers (to help with bruising... in Texas you can find these packaged in Mexican markets)
- Burdock root (used by the Amish for wound healing)
- Calendula flowers (this is what Serafine uses for bee stings and ant bites)
- Cayenne powder (for arthritis)
- Chamomile flowers (soothing... can be mixed with calendula... also available at most Mexican markets)
- Ginger root (for sore muscles)
- Yarrow leaves and flowers (for wound healing)

ABOUT THE AUTHOR

Karen MacInerney is the *USA Today* bestselling author of multiple mystery series, and her victims number well into the double digits. She lives in quaint Georgetown, Texas with her sassy family, Tristan, Little Bit, and a new arrival, a Chihuahua rescue named Iggy (a.k.a. Dog #1, Dog #2, and Dog #3).

Feel free to visit Karen's web site at www. karenmacinerney.com, where you can download a free book and sign up for her Readers' Circle to receive subscriber-only short stories, deleted scenes, recipes and other bonus material. You can also find her on Facebook (she spends an inordinate amount of time there), where Karen loves getting to know her readers, answering questions, and offering quirky, behind-the-scenes looks at the writing process (and life in general).

P. S. Don't forget to follow Karen on BookBub to get news-flashes on new releases!

www.karenmacinerney.com
karen@karenmacinerney.com

facebook.com/AuthorKarenMacInerney

Made in the USA
Coppell, TX
08 January 2021